DOUBLE TIME

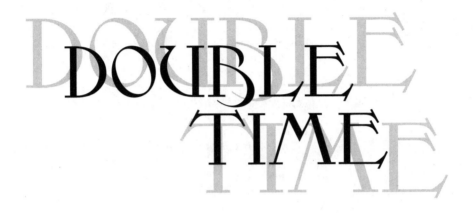

DOUBLE TIME

A NOVEL BY

PRISCILLA COGAN

TWO CANOES PRESS
Hopkinton, Massachusetts

Two Canoes Press
PO Box 334
Hopkinton, MA 01748
www.TwoCanoesPress.com

Cover and book design by Arrow Graphics, Inc.
Watertown, Massachusetts
info@arrow1.com

Cover illustration by Kristin Hurlin
Author's photograph by Duncan Sings-Alone

Manufactured in the United States of America

Publisher's Cataloging-in-Publication
(Provided by Quality Books, Inc.)

Cogan, Priscilla, 1947-
Double time : a novel / by Priscilla Cogan.
p.   cm.
LCCN 2006932221
ISBN-13: 978-1-929590-07-0
ISBN-10: 1-929590-07-5

1. Change (Psychology)—Fiction. 2. Identity
(Psychology)—Fiction. 3. Books and reading—
Psychological aspects—Fiction. 4. Literature—
Psychological aspects—Fiction. 5. Kidnapping—Fiction.
6. Travelers—Fiction. 7. Psychological fiction.
8. Adventure fiction.   I. Title.

PS3553.O4152D69 2007   813'.54
                QBI06-600334

ACKNOWLEDGMENTS

First of all, I want to thank the readers of my previous three novels in *The Winona Series* who have written from all over the world detailing the impact that my novels have had upon their lives. That feedback resulted in this story of a novel within a novel.

A book always emerges from the collective efforts of several contributors. I am grateful for the stunning cover art of Kristin Hurlin, the wonderful design elements of Alvart Badalian of Arrow Graphics Inc., and the helpful editorial work of Mary C. Babl of Hummingbird Editing.

My thanks to Will Bain for guiding me through a pictorial description of the Northwest passages I have not yet traveled, to F. Earle Beaton for providing me accurate information on firearms, and to Evelyn Wolfson for her grammatical suggestions.

As always, I am incredibly dependent on the support of two individuals: my husband and my sister.

My sister, Polly Parson, keeps me grounded to personal history and laughs with me about the passage of time through the body.

My husband, Duncan Sings-Alone, is simply and profoundly my best friend and muse.

Dedication

For Laura McKelvey and Wendy Parciak,

One a teller of tales.

One a writer of stories.

"Storytelling helps keep the world spinning in the right direction."

—Eth-Noh-Tec

"A story is the shortest distance between people."

—Pat Speight

ONE

WASHINGTON, D.C.

It was one of those days when nothing goes right. One of those days when the wind throws grit into the human eye and, in a blink, the world shifts and shivers and nothing is the same as it was. When life itself blurs out of focus and, in the void, echoes the great belly laugh of the universe.

On this day, Billy T. Pickle desperately hoped he could solve his most pressing problem—to win back the affections of his wife, Carmelita.

All of thirteen years old, Phoenix Knott decided that this was *THE* day to run away from home, certain that her absentee father in Seattle would welcome her with open arms and no rules.

And, without a shred of doubt, the widow Kate Aregood knew that this day would be like all the rest:

Boringly predictable.

It started out well enough. After digesting a cup of bran cereal with skim milk, Kate shooed her late husband's cat Poofie outside, gathered up her keys, and triple-locked the townhouse front door. Once inside her ancient, powder blue Dodge Dart, she held down the accelerator four seconds before turning on the motor. The car lurched forward, back lights blinking, as Kate pumped the brakes all the way down the street.

It was one of those hot Washington summer days, when even Congress has the sense to pack up and go home.

In the air-conditioned, spotless lobby of The National Trust Bank, Phoenix Knott tucked the sum total of her babysitting money into a leather pouch hanging off her neck, adjusted her mirrored sunglasses and headphones, clipped the white iPod to her jeans, and hoisted an overstuffed backpack onto her back. Sprouting from the rear of her Redskins cap, her blond pony tail bounced to rap rhythms.

To Billy Pickle's dismay, there were no available parking spaces near The National Trust Bank, except one occupied by two teenage boys gutter-kicking a soccer ball. Slowly, he angled Carmelita's car into the space, forcing the boys to relinquish the spot.

"Scuzbag," one growled at him.

"Fartface," the other chorused.

With his most disarming, self-effacing smile, he raised a hand in greeting.

They both gave him the finger.

Stowing Carmelita's grocery list in one pocket, Billy looked at himself in the rearview mirror, checking to make sure that he had appropriately positioned the fake black mustache, reflective sunglasses, and brown wig. He slid an antique, thirty-eight caliber pistol into a paper sack, grabbed a green plastic bag, thrust them under his arm, and exited the car. Under the hostile glare of the teenagers, he fed the parking meter, calculating that his business at the bank would take him no more than fifteen minutes. Perspiration trickled down his face and neck.

The drumming of his heart catapulted into fast jazz rhythms as he paused before the massive, revolving bank doors, all metal and glass. He could simply walk away. No harm done. But the moment to retreat skittered by. *A man's gotta do what a man's gotta do.* Billy sucked in his gut and thrust out his chest. He shoved the revolving door, the back of which thwacked him hard on his shoulders, launching him toward his manifest destiny.

Billy spotted, then advanced toward the pretty cashier with no customers. *An easy mark.* Aware of sweat and slippage, he fingered the mustache, pressing it hard onto his upper lip. In the paper bag, he palmed the gun with his right hand, a smooth move he had practiced at home. With his left hand, he pulled out the list of his demands, thrust it toward the cashier with the green sack, and positioned the gun in line with her ample breasts. Any moment now, he expected her eyes to enlarge with terror.

His note, written earlier that morning, warned:

This is a holdup. I got a gun. Fill the grean bag with money.

The cashier scanned the piece of paper before her:

white rice, black beans
1 lb. pork tenderloin
8 large tomatoes, green chilies
espresso coffee beans
cream, eggs, pure stick butter
hickory smoked bacon!!!!!
cappuccino ice cream
a baguette
hypoallegenic face cream, black eyebrow pencil
chocolate almond roca
7 grain bread machine mix
8 black candles

At first she looked puzzled, then smiled sweetly at him. Billy nodded and shoved the paper bag toward her.

Something was wrong.

Her smile wasn't dissolving into panic. Instead, her eyes softened with compassionate understanding. She tapped her ear and spoke with exaggerated slowness, "Are you deaf?"

"Huh?"

She turned over the note he had given her and drew several *?????*.

Dumbfounded, he stared at the question marks.

Flipping the note, he stabbed at it with his digit finger to reinforce his potential for violence.

In pantomime, she tapped the list with her finger. Right above the words *rice and beans*.

Rice and beans!

"I gave you the wrong, the wrong thing-a-ma-jig," he sputtered. The threatening note fluttered in his hand, as he whipped it out of his pocket and pushed it toward her.

Before picking it up, the young woman giggled. "I didn't know you could talk."

She read:

This is a holdup. I got a gun. Fill the grean bag with money.

"This is a joke, yes?"

"No. It isn't." As he shook his head, the wig began to slip. Time was slinking up on him. Already, a line behind him was beginning to form. A male executive across the lobby eyed him suspiciously.

"Don't trip the alarm," he whispered, rustling the gun in the paper sack. "Just put the money in the bag." He grabbed the note of demands and stuffed it back into his pocket.

She moved slowly, much too slowly, emptying her cash drawer. Ones, fives, and twenties. It wasn't much. He suspected that her feet, which he could not see, were stomping on a silent alarm.

"More?" she asked him.

As if he were a customer needing a second cup of coffee.

He looked at the bank clock. His time was up. He shook his head.

The cashier slid the bag and leaned her lovely breasts over the counter. "You better run quick. Your mustache is about to peel off."

In the distant streets, he could hear the police sirens howl their prophetic wail. Up on the wall, the video camera was scanning his face for posterity.

"I'm sorry. I hope I didn't scare you none," he whispered. It seemed the right thing to say. He grabbed the green bag, still covering his pistol hand.

"Excuse me, please," he said as he buzzed past a waiting line of depositors. Any moment now, he expected the bank doors to lock shut, trap him forever, but no one seemed to be paying him any attention.

Outside, the sirens grew louder, a deafening wail of doom. Out the bank door he propelled himself. In a moment of desperation or sheer stupidity, he later surmised, the idea of taking a hostage flashed into his brain. An impulsive decision, meant only to serve as a temporary solution.

Wired to headphones and heading for the bus station, Phoenix Knott couldn't hear the howling of approaching police cars.

From years of watching Jimmy Cagney films, Billy knew exactly what to do. Running up behind the girl, he shoved the pistol into her side. "Do what I say an' you won't get hurt."

"What?" she screeched.

"Do what I say an' you won't get hurt."

"Hey," she yelled at him. The look she gave him was one of disgust, as if loose snot was spewing from his nose.

"Do what I say," he repeated a third time, then yanked off her earphones, "an' you won't get hurt. I gotta gun."

"I don't care if you have a gun, a knife, or you're a kung fu champion. Get your friggin' hands offa me." She elbowed him in the side.

"Oof," he exhaled, then grabbed her wrist, before she could do it again. Only a block away now, the sirens and cops were coming for him.

She kicked his ankle.

"Ouch. Quit it," he yelled, hopping on one foot.

She wouldn't stop wiggling, but Billy was strong and had a good grip on her.

"Look," he said, "I'm in really deep shit, and I need your help. I promise I won't hurt you." He whipped off his wig, mustache, and glasses, while keeping a steady hand upon her. "Here, stuff these in your jacket."

"It'll make me look fat," she protested.

"Please." He gave her the most appealing hangdog look and let go her wrist.

It worked.

She sighed, took the articles, and jammed them in her windbreaker.

"Now I'm going to take your arm, as if we're father and daughter."

"Pul-leaze, you're not my father."

A few hundred feet behind them, a police car ran up over the curb. Then a second and a third, disgorging the men in blue. Guns drawn, they scrambled, one after another, into the bank. A weird, inexplicable, maternal attitude suddenly flooded Phoenix. Something about Billy was like a bird with a broken wing or an orphaned puppy dog. She took his arm and gently urged him away from the cavalcade of arriving police cars.

"Just to the end of the block," she cautioned, not wanting him to get any strange ideas.

An odd fatigue settled over him, as he gave way to the feminine tug. All his life it had been like this. Women wanting to take care of him.

That is, until Carmelita.

"My car's right there." He nodded toward the white automobile. On the periphery of his vision, he noted the two teenage boys sidling away from the automobile, whistling.

"Your tires are flat." She was the first to spot the damage.

"No." He couldn't believe it. Both curbside tires, slashed and punctured. His eyes shifted toward the boys' backs retreating down the street.

One of the boys thrust a fist in the air and shouted, "Yesss!"

"Damn." Billy shook his head. Carmelita wasn't going to like this one bit. It was her car.

Phoenix nudged him. "Now, whatcha going to do?"

Behind him, he could hear the commotion at the bank. A surge of adrenaline slammed into his system. Grabbing Phoenix's hand, he pulled her into a fast trot on the sidewalk, away from the bank.

"Hey, hey. Lemme go," she protested.

That was when he spotted a powder blue car braking its way down the street.

"Yes, indeedy." He half-ran, half-dragged the teenager towards the Dodge Dart. The car was going so slowly that it took little effort to wrench open the front door and shove in the girl. He jumped into the back seat.

Leveling the gun's barrel at the back of the driver's head, he yelled, "Step on it."

The white-haired driver slammed on the brakes.

"I have a gun aimed at your head, an' I'm not afraid to use it. Now move," he snarled.

"Absolutely not," the female driver answered.

Two police vehicles, heading for the bank, split around the car, their sirens blaring.

The Dodge Dart didn't budge.

"What?" Billy was incredulous. Did this woman want to die?

"Absolutely not," the woman repeated, "until the two of you buckle up. I never drive my car without everyone strapping on their seat belts." Only when she turned her head around to give him a beady stare did he realize how ancient she was. Older than Methuselah.

Behind them, a couple of drivers stuck their heads out the windows, gesturing and honking.

"Okay, okay. Put on your seat belt," he ordered Phoenix, while scrambling to fasten his own. He tried a more mannerly approach. "Done. Now, please, can we get going?"

"Certainly," the woman answered, pumping the accelerator. The car lurched to life, tires protesting.

Billy's only thought was to put as much distance between himself and the bank, to get out of the city, out of the state.

"Head north," he ordered. The woman's driving was jerky, but who was he to complain? At this point, any vehicle would do. He couldn't believe his good luck in having hijacked a Dodge Dart. For if there was one thing Billy knew, it was old cars.

Past the Smithsonian museums, along Independence Ave, Kate Aregood drove at a slow but steady pace

"Keep to the Potomac," he said. His Mama had always told him that if he ever got lost, follow the river. *Gotta ditch these two women as soon as I can an' keep the car*, he reasoned. He regretted not having worked out alternative escape plans.

My, oh my, this day is turning out to be quite different, thought Kate, both hands clutching the wheel. *A desperate gunman, a terrified girl, a car hijacking. What am I going to do?*

Cruising by the Kennedy Center and the Watergate complex, she braked sharply at a red light. A white police car pulled up alongside, a golden opportunity for Kate to put an end to this desperado's escape, play the heroine, and save herself and the teenager from grievous harm. To signal their imminent danger, she needed to attract the policeman's attention. Mimicking the gargoyles that sit atop the National Cathedral, her beloved Episcopalian church, Kate grimaced and warped her face in the policeman's direction. Her eyebrows gyrated up and down. Her lips puckered, pouted, and pointed towards the man in her back seat, but without any sound to alert Billy to what she was doing.

The police officer finally took notice of her. He smiled and tipped his hat.

No. That wasn't what she wanted. Kate redoubled her efforts with facial expressions of concern, worry, and fear.

The police officer leaned out his window frame, as if planning to ask her what was the matter.

Taking a risk, she nodded vigorously to him, then again arched her eyebrows back toward Billy.

"Don't try anything stupid," whispered Billy from the back seat.

"Or you'll get us all killed," echoed Phoenix.

The light turned green.

The cop smiled, replaced his hat upon his head. His car peeled off to the right, up Virginia Ave.

Billy gave him a friendly wave.

Phoenix Knott hunkered down in the front seat, hand upon the door handle, ready to jump out at the first opportunity. The only problem was that Billy had locked her door. This guy might be a pervert or a serial killer, someone featured on America's Most Wanted show. She couldn't care less what Billy did to the perfumed old woman, but she didn't want to hurt herself or her iPod by leaping out of a moving car.

"Do you gotta road atlas?" Billy asked, as the Dodge Dart swung up Rock Creek Parkway.

"Of course, I do. It's under the seat where the young lady is sitting."

"My name's Phoenix."

"And mine is Kate." The elderly woman took her eyes and right hand off the steering wheel and held it out to shake Phoenix's hand, but the teenager pretended not to notice. The car heaved to the left of the yellow line then ricochet back across their lane.

"Hey," the girl shouted. "Pay attention to your driving!"

"Listen," scolded Billy. "There's no reason to get rude. You gotta respect your elders."

"And your name is?" Kate peered into the rearview mirror.

"William. But everybody calls me Billy." He started to reach over to shake Kate's hand, but his hand was still clutching the pistol.

Kate steadied her grip on the wheel, keeping her eyes focused on the road.

Billy pointed the gun at Phoenix. "Find the map, will you?"

Phoenix sighed, as if asked to do some monumental task. She adjusted her earphones.

Billy jabbed her in the shoulder with his pistol. "Now," he ordered.

"Whatever." She pulled the map out from under her seat and handed it back to him. *Creep.*

Painfully, he studied the map. He had always found the crisscrossing patchwork of blue and red roads confusing.

"Head for Interstate 270." Although it might be dangerous to travel the interstate he had to get out of the District of Columbia as quick as possible. *Oh, shit. I gotta call Carmelita an' tell her where to find the car. She's gonna tar and feather me about those tires and the groceries. The grocery list.* What had he done with Carmelita's grocery list? He fished into both pockets but could only find the threatening note. *Oh, she'll be madder than a wet hen.* Even though she had kicked him out the day he lost his factory job, she still expected him to do the food shopping.

"Bee-ly," she had said, "it's not that I don't love you, but you make no money for us. Be a man for once, Bee-ly. You come home when you get a steady job." Carmelita knew what she wanted.

"May I ask you, what are your intentions?" Kate asked.

"Yeah," said Phoenix, "Are you planning to shoot us?"

"I told you—" he began.

"Or maybe stab us and cut us to pieces?" the teenager added.

"That's not my—"

"Or lock us in the trunk so that we die of starvation."

"No," he answered.

"Yeah, you probably just want to rape us and take all our money."

"What?" Billy stared at her. "What is your problem?"

"Maybe," the youngster elaborated, "you've already dug a secret grave in the forest and you're going to dump us in it and ask our relatives for ransom. Maybe you think we're rich and you can make a lot of money, but we'd die of suffocation and—"

"Hush," said Kate.

"Shut up," echoed Billy. He could hardly think for all the teenager's racket. "Look, I . . . I really don't know. Something will come to me."

"Well," admonished Kate, "she does have a point. In a few minutes, we'll be entering Maryland. It's a federal crime to rob banks. Soon you'll be adding kidnaping across state lines. The Federal Bureau of Investigation will have to get involved."

Kate had great faith in the F.B.I. She wanted Billy to be aware of the consequences of his reckless actions.

"The F.B.I.," squealed Phoenix. "Then we'll be famous. On the radio. On television."

Billy, however, was much more fearful of Carmelita than the F.B.I. "She's gonna to kill me."

"Who?" Kate asked.

Phoenix switched on the car radio.

Before he could answer, an announcer's voice boomed forth from the car's speaker:

. . . National Trust Bank robbery but no one was hurt. Witnesses say that the criminal is a white male, about twenty-five years old, five feet eleven inches tall, and weighing approximately two hundred pounds. He left on foot, disappearing into the surrounding neighborhood. A house to house search is currently being conducted. That is all the information that we have at this time. Now onto other news . . .

Phoenix flipped off the station and frowned at Kate. "That's all? There's nothing about us."

"They made me shorter and fatter. Younger too." Managing a wan smile, Billy added, "Must be my good looks."

"They'll soon discover that you've taken hostages." Although Kate spoke with great authority, she knew that nobody but Poofie would notice her absence for several days. And even that might be giving Poofie too much credit.

"Yeah." Phoenix puffed right up. "And when my Dad catches you, he's going to beat the living shit out of you. He's going to hunt you down like a dirty dawg and kick butt big-time."

But it wasn't Phoenix's father and it wasn't the F.B.I. that caused Billy's heart to surge in panic. It was the image of his beloved Carmelita, her beautiful black hair whipping off her shoulders, her deep brown eyes pinched small and fiery, her bright red mouth scrunched up and screaming at him, "Bee-ly, estupido! You are a cock-a-roach of a man. A man without huevos. You are nada, Bee-ly. Nothing you do is EVER EVER right!"

TWO

MARYLAND

"Welcome to Maryland!" signs dotted the road. Billy had now committed his second federal offense: kidnaping across state lines. Probably life in prison, if caught. The way he figured it, he better keep on going. Only he didn't know where. Planning out future strategies had never been one of his strengths. He'd just have to take it one state at a time.

A lot of *if onlys* careened across his brain:

If only he hadn't messed up the bank robbery with the grocery list.

If only the two delinquents hadn't flattened his tires.

If only Carmelita hadn't thrown him out of the apartment.

If only he could have been a better husband.

He hung his head under the heavy burden of his failures.

Meanwhile, Kate pumped on by the shopping districts of Rockville, heading north as Billy had instructed. Her mind was busy, working out possible escape scenarios. Much to her relief, Billy had tucked the pistol out of sight.

Phoenix quickly grew restless in the vacuum of their respective silences. She readjusted her headphones and switched on her iPod. Nothing happened. Damn, the charge had run down. She should have bought a charger before hitting the road. She stared incredulously at the front console.

"How am I ever going to survive?" She thumped the dashboard in frustration.

"Please respect my property, young lady," Kate said.

"Phoenix. I told you, my name is Phoenix."

"Phoenix it is. The name of my car happens to be Matilda, and Matilda does not like it when rude young people feel compelled to pound on her." Kate didn't relish the task of having to teach this teenager elementary manners. Parents simply were not doing an adequate job these days.

"This old bucket has a name? Gimme a break," Phoenix said. Nobody seemed to understand how she was suffocating, stuck in the front seat with an elderly fussbudget whose flowery perfume choked the air and a crazy man in the back.

"I . . . I like that name," Billy chimed in from the back seat. "Don't pay her no mind. It's a great car."

"Why, thank you, Billy." Obviously, he wasn't really such a bad man, just misguided. Maybe he simply needed a friendly soul to help set him on the right path.

"I've gotta stop," declared the teenager. "I'm hungry and I gotta go."

It wasn't exactly the truth. What Phoenix wanted most of all was to get away from the pervert and the old lady. If that wasn't possible, then, at the very least, to buy a charger for her iPod. It was the only way she was going to be able to make it through the next few hours and not freak out.

Outside, the crowded suburban landscape was yielding to more spacious, rural views. Dairy farms and rolling hills slid on by, as the cities of Washington and Rockville sank below the back horizon. Billy could see that the Dodge Dart was going to need fuel before too long.

"Pull off that exit." He pointed to the right. A country fruit stand/gas station was positioned right off the interstate. Kate did as she was told, finally stopping the car under the station's overhang.

Pocketing the pistol, Billy accompanied the two women to the restroom area. "I'll be waiting outside. Don't try nuthin' funny."

Kate's legs and feet felt stiff from the driving. It was not her habit to take Matilda out on long trips. She was simply getting too old for this. Maybe she could persuade Billy to take the wheel for awhile.

Phoenix scouted the restroom area for an escape route. "There's only that small window, and that creep is standing out by the door." She entered a dirty stall. Might as well do her business while there was the opportunity. "I can go all day without using the bathroom if I have to," she boasted.

"Well, I can't," Kate answered from the other stall.

Outside, Billy danced from one foot to another, wary about leaving his post but needing to pee in the worst way. Finally, he dashed into the men's room. By the time he returned to the outside, the women were still loitering in the restroom.

It never failed to amaze him how long it took females to do their thing in the bathroom.

As they emerged, he directed them to the fruit stand and bought several plums, bananas, and apples. "That should keep us going awhile," he announced.

"I don't eat fruit," Phoenix said.

"Fruit causes me indigestion and other problems," Kate added. "Perhaps we can find a restaurant?"

It was a question Billy chose not to answer.

"Well then. Maybe later," she said.

Billy shrugged his shoulders and hefted the bag of fruit. Sometimes, there was simply no pleasing women. At least he'd enjoy the apples. He filled up the car with gas and paid the attendant with the bank money. He kept the keys in his pocket, along with the gun. There was no way that the two gals could drive away without him.

"If you don't mind, I'd like to take a break from driving," Kate said.

"No ma'am. I need you to drive." All the better to keep his eyes on the two of them in the front seat.

"I know how to drive," Phoenix interjected.

The two adults didn't respond.

Kate sighed and resumed her place in the driver's seat.

Billy didn't trust them. No telling what kind of escape plans they'd been hatching in the ladies' room.

And, indeed, they had.

In a moment of rare self-revelation, Phoenix had divulged to Kate that she had run away from home that morning and, therefore, would not be missed. "I left Mom a note, telling her where I was going and how. I said I would call her when I arrived at my Dad's house. She knows I can take care of myself."

Kate had reassured her. "Now don't you worry. I'll think of something. Sometimes, one simply has to wait for the right moment to present itself. Probably the best strategy you and I could devise would be to keep our eyes open for that singular occasion. It will come sooner or later. Remember, Billy is just a man. He has to eat and go to sleep like all the rest of us human beings. It is when his attention wanders that we'll be able to make our break. There's only one problem that I foresee."

"What's that?" Maybe the old lady wasn't so bad. You had to give her credit. She wasn't wacked out or hysterical as some other people might have been in this situation.

"Well," Kate confessed. "I'm loath to run away and leave my Matilda in the hands of a common crook. But we do what we have to do. I think she would understand."

Frankly, Matilda didn't seem to care as long as her metal belly was full and a human foot was pressing the accelerator. She flew past the city of Frederick, heading up route 15 toward Thurmont, the Catoctin mountains, and Camp David. Billy anointed the passing scenery with banana peels, apple cores, and plum pits.

"That's gross," Phoenix said. "Why can't you wait for the trash can?"

"Squirrels can't eat 'em then," Billy answered, "an' squirrels gotta eat and get fat, so I can shoot 'em and cook 'em up."

"Oh super gross." Phoenix jabbed a finger in her mouth, as if to vomit.

"Silence is golden," Kate said.

"All right." Phoenix flipped on the car radio and began to hunt down news reports. To her great dismay, there was nothing about the bank robbery. The local news focused on the price of hay and grains. She scoured the channels for some decent music. The radio bass boomed out:

> *Thunka, thunka, thun Kaa*
> *Thunka, thunka, thun Kaa*
> *Thunka, thunka, thun Kaa*

"Yeah." Phoenix rocked against the seat.

> *I tole that gal to kiss my ass*
> *That sistah, she has got the sass*
> *I do not need no mouthy ho'*
> *To tell me where and how to go*
>
> *Thunka, thunka, thun Kaa*
> *Thunka, thunka, thun Kaa*
> *Thunka, thunka, thun Kaa*

"What?" Kate leaned forward to listen. She couldn't believe her ears.

> *Got to find a sweet meat honey,*
> *Bitch with no itch for Daddy's money*
> *I'm through with all her flash cash fits*
> *I want the love without the shit!*

Thunka, thunka, thun Kaa
Thunka, thunka, thun Kaa
Thunka, thunka, thun Kaa

"No!" exclaimed Kate, fumbling to twist off the radio switch. "That's the most disgusting . . ."

"Hey, I was listening to that," Phoenix protested. As she reached over to turn it back on, Kate slapped away her hand.

"No means No." Kate's face twisted into gargoyle proportions.

"Shit fuck," Phoenix yelled.

Kate gasped. Her face turned apoplectic red.

Before it could turn into a cat fight, Billy leaned over the back seat and twisted the dial to a country music station.

A languorous sound of guitars and synthesizer soothed the ruffled air.

I'm a-walking down the street
Listening to the city's beat
Watching lonely people cry
By themselves, the world flies by,
And my heart, it breaks in two
When I think of me and you.

Baby, honey, sweetie-pea
Please come back to sorry me.

I'm a-winging in the air,
Like a bird that soars nowhere,
Circling currents in the storm
Knowing all has come to harm

And my heart, it flies in two
When I think of me and you.

Baby, honey, sweetie-pea
Please come back to sorry me.

I'm a-drifting in the brine
You, the mermaid in my mind.
Promised for eternal years
Drowning now, a flood of tears,
And my heart, it breaks in two
When I think of me and you.

Baby, honey, sweetie-pea
Please come back to sorry me.

O-o-o-o, Baby, baby, baby
O-o-o-o, Honey, honey, honey
O-o-o-o, Sweetie-pea
Come back, come back
To sorry sorry me.

"Now, isn't that a whole lot better?" Billy said.

"It isn't fair that you get to hear what you want and I can't," Phoenix said, "and besides, that music is pure mush. Like—"

"Whipped cream on top of melted marshmallows," Kate interjected.

"Yes," agreed Phoenix.

"Well, I can't stand that rap crap." Billy sulked. "Find something else then." He slumped back into his seat.

Kate turned the channel to the public broadcasting station where, in a high-nosed voice that bespoke culture beyond the masses, the announcer intoned, ". . . his magnificent Fifth Symphony."

> *Da da da dum*
> *Da da da dum*
> *Da da da, da da da, da da da . . .*

Beethoven's masterpiece. Kate's face shifted into a trance-like state. Phoenix donned her earphones to block the sound. Only after the second movement did Kate turn down the volume to await their opinions.

But Phoenix had drifted off asleep, and Billy was staring out the window, dreaming of Carmelita and humming "sorry sorry me." Seeing his mournful face reflected in the rear view mirror, Kate didn't have the heart to inform him that they had just crossed over into Pennsylvania.

THREE

PENNSYLVANIA

Unfriendly signs greeted them upon entry into Pennsylvania. If they were caught speeding, the fines would be exorbitant. Kate slowed Matilda to fifty miles per hour.

Billy raised his head from studying the map. "Drive along the Susquehanna River when you come to it." *Follow the river, son.*

Past York, the broad body of water came into view, a tumbling river dotted with boulders and laced with bridges. The afternoon sun glinted off its surface, reminding Kate of childhood: brooks, stepping stones, and the magic of walking across water without getting one's feet wet. The fatigue of the driving sank onto her shoulders, a dull but not unpleasant ache. "My goodness, it's been years since I've been to Pennsylvania."

"I need to stop," Phoenix announced. "My iPod won't work. You won't let me listen to rap on the radio, so I gotta get a car charger for it."

"No," Billy answered. They were still too close to D.C.

"No," Kate echoed. She couldn't imagine how Phoenix's mother ever let her listen to such trash.

"No?" Phoenix eyes narrowed.

"No," repeated Billy. "Now shut up and lemme think."

"No?" Phoenix's voice shot back.

He glared at her. "Now, don't you go getting me all riled up."

Phoenix leaned forward. "Then I'm going to turn on the radio."

"Let's take a vote," suggested Kate. "We live in a democratic society. The majority can decide what kind of music the radio will play."

"Do I even get to vote?" Phoenix squirreled up her mouth.

"Of course," snapped Kate. "Now all those in favor of listening to rap music, raise your hand."

Only Phoenix's hand touched the air.

"Well, that's decisive," said Kate.

"All those wantin' country music, raise yer hands." Billy couldn't believe it when his was the only hand in the air.

"So, I guess it's classical music then." Kate smiled.

"No. Gotta vote on that too," Phoenix said. "All those in favor of the uppity music, raise your hands."

Eyes on the road, Kate carefully took her right hand off the wheel. Billy and Phoenix kept their arms pinned to their sides.

"Ah ha," chortled Phoenix. "Checkmate."

"So the thing-a-ma-jig stays off," Billy said.

"You mean the radio?" Phoenix couldn't believe how dumb this guy was.

"Yeah, that's what I mean."

"Then why don't you say it? Ra-di-o."

"I just forgot the word. Okay?"

"We need to stop bickering and find some place to eat," Kate said. "Our blood sugar is running low, and that's what's making all of us so irritable. Besides, I've driven more today than I have in years. Frankly, I'm tired. You'll have to take the wheel soon." Kate checked her rearview mirror.

"Okay, okay," he agreed. "Jus' promise me you won't try to escape or nuthin.'" To make a point, he pulled out his pistol and waved it at the two of them.

"All right, but put that pistol away," Kate said. The gun made her nervous. You never could tell when one of them might accidentally discharge.

On the outskirts of Harrisburg, he directed her to a parking space near a small outdoor cafe. "We'll eat here, then I'll drive." Inside the restaurant, he positioned himself briefly by the ladies room before scurrying to the men's room.

"He's gone," Phoenix whispered, having cracked opened the restroom door. "Let's get out of here before he kills us."

"I can't," Kate answered, washing her hands.

"Huh? Are you crazy? He's gone, I tell you."

"I gave my word. My word means something." Kate dried her hands on the revolving towel rack.

"Look, he's dangerous. Like he's got a gun. He's probably planning to murder us when it's dark. So let's go."

Kate shook her head.

"Are you crazy?"

"I gave my word not to run, but you didn't. So if you want to leave, go while he's occupied elsewhere. I'll try to distract him."

Phoenix grabbed the door handle. "When I get far enough away, I'll tell the cops. Okay?" It was the least she could do. She opened the door, checked to make sure the way was clear, and took off.

Kate emerged from the women's room, just as Billy exited the men's room.

"Where's the kid?"

"I think she just made her escape." Kate pointed in the opposite direction of Phoenix's getaway.

His shoulders sagged, as he stared out the window, down the empty side road. It would simply be a matter of time before the police would know his identity, a full description of the car, and details of the kidnaping and bank robbery. Soon they would descend upon him, read him his rights, probably rough him up some, then snap him in handcuffs, line him up with murderers for a mug shot, jam his fingertips onto an inkpad, and toss him in the cooler with homosexual rapists. Immobilized, he stood there, one foot pointed to the outside door, the other toward the restaurant area.

"She's gone. I don't think you can catch her. Let's have a bite to eat, shall we?" Kate took his arm and guided him into the dark-lit restaurant. No one could make a good decision without proper nourishment.

It would probably be his last good meal. He could run to the car and make an escape but what was the use? They'd have his name, his picture, and the car description on television in no time flat. They'd say he was "armed and dangerous," probably shoot him to save the taxpayers the trouble of a trial. *I'm not ready to die*, he thought.

While he picked at his hamburger and fries, he was amazed to see how much the old lady was able to eat. Beginning with a bowl of tomato soup topped with garlic croutons, she consumed a salad of mixed greens, a generous serving of chicken pot pie, and a cup of decaffeinated coffee.

He kept turning his head toward the door, expecting the cops to arrive. His stomach churned.

When the waitress asked them if they wanted dessert, Kate shook her head. The young woman handed him the bill. He pulled out a small stash of money from his pocket. He hadn't even counted how much he'd made from the robbery. Somehow, the amount no longer seemed all that important in light of the enormity of his crimes. He left the waitress a large tip. She seemed like a nice woman. *Maybe she'll speak up and say something sweet to the police when they question her. Like "he was a nice enough guy. Gave a big tip."*

He opened the restaurant door cautiously. No sign of cops anywhere. *Maybe it's going to be okay. Maybe this will turn out to be my lucky day.* Certainly it was a stroke of good luck to get rid of the teenager. She'd begun to grate on his nerves big time. *But why hasn't she contacted the police? Maybe she's afraid, still running down the road, thinking I'm gonna come after her and hurt her. If only she knew . . .*

"Bee-ly, you can't even keel a fly," Carmelita used to say. Another one of his many shortcomings.

Billy stopped short of the Dodge Dart and eyed Kate suspiciously. "Why didn't you run too? Was it the car?"

"I gave you my word."

Suddenly, he yanked out his gun, whispering, "Someone's in the car."

He jerked open the door. "Okay, whoever you are, raise your hands before I blow your friggin' head off."

Up went the hands but down went the head.

"Hush. That's no policeman," said Kate. "It's Phoenix. Now put down that gun."

Billy should have been relieved, but he wasn't. Although the police had obviously not been alerted, he was still going to have to deal with the girl.

Kate opened the back door, sat down, and slammed shut the door. She had no intention of driving anymore that day.

Sheepishly, Phoenix looked at Kate. "I didn't know where to go. I can't go home. I'll just get in trouble. I want to see my Dad. I didn't know what to do. I thought he might shoot me."

Hands still aloft, she looked at Billy's gun. "I didn't tell the police or nothing. That's the truth."

"I believe you." Kate turned toward Billy. "Now put down that gun." It was as close to an order as she dared give him.

"I dunno." Billy got into the driver's seat, the gun still aimed at Phoenix's chest. "You done irritate me to no end. Why did you come back?" It came out more as a complaint than a question.

Phoenix kept her eyes focused on the pistol's barrel. "I was scared of you coming after me."

"That makes no sense at all." He thrust the gun closer. "You be straight with me, you hear?"

"I need a ride. To Seattle. Or as close as I can get."

"You wanna free ride? That's why you come back?"

Phoenix nodded but curled away from the gun as far as she could get.

"You know you're crazy, don'tcha?" He shook his head, lowered the gun, and stowed it back in his pocket. "You're a crazy runaway, that's what you are."

Kate's heart was thumping fast and loud. For a moment there, she thought he was going to lose it, kill the two of them, and take off.

"Okay," he said, looking into the rearview mirror. "What about you?"

"Yes?"

"If you run off, I'll have to kill the girl, you understand? I'll hunt her down like a dirty dawg, if either one of you leave. I don't want to do it, but that's jus' the way it is. We're all in this together."

Kate bit her lip and nodded.

"Will you promise not to run?"

Again, she nodded.

"Okay, this is our new plan." He addressed them both, pleased at how clear he sounded. "When I'm ready to go it alone, I'll drop you both off at the nearest bus station. Nobody gets hurt that way. Agreed?"

"Agreed," said Kate. The sooner the better.

"Only one problem," said Phoenix.

His heart sank. Was there no end to this teenager's complaints? "What's that?"

"You're headed north. I want to go west."

"Look, I'm jus' following the river for awhile. Then I'll head west. Okay?"

"Okay."

That seemed easy enough. Billy sighed with relief. No longer would he have to closely guard them. Having scared the living daylights outta the two women, he could take his time at the urinals and nap in the car when tired. He revved up the car's engine.

Kate could feel her pulse slowly return to normal. She must not act afraid. She must be cool-headed and composed to protect the girl and herself. He was armed and dangerous. She had been foolish not to escape earlier with Phoenix. Always trusting people to do the right thing. *He could have killed us.*

I must remain calm, she thought, remembering the Yoga instructions. *Calmness is a state of deep, slow, and meditative breathing.* Kate closed her eyes, inhaled and exhaled slowly, inhaled, then exhaled, until the day's events caught up to her. She fell asleep.

As Billy rediscovered the pleasure of driving a Dodge Dart, Phoenix spent the next half hour sitting unnaturally still. Her initial burst of terror morphed into common fear, then curiosity, then boredom, an itch that needed to be scratched, then plain discomfort. It was impossible to maintain a position of immobility for long. Only after checking to make sure Kate's eyes were closed did she shuck off her shoes and splay her toes upon the blue dashboard.

Whether it was the scratching of bare toes on vinyl or the sweaty smell of feet on the sun-hot dashboard, something twitched Kate's eyelids half-open. "Matilda does not appreciate the imprint of bare feet."

Phoenix dropped her feet and turned to look at Kate, but the eyelids had already shut again. A satisfied smiled sat upon the old woman's face.

As the afternoon sun began to sink towards Seattle, Matilda easily glided up the Susquehanna River valley, finally pulling over into a Holiday Inn at Williamsport, the home of Little League. The town was packed for the Little League World Series.

"There are three of us," said Billy to the motel clerk.

"Sorry. Only one room is left. Two double beds." The clerk shrugged his shoulders.

Once in the room, Phoenix flopped on both beds, before choosing the one with the softest mattress. "This one is mine," she proclaimed. The teenager observed Billy eyeing the other bed. "No way, Jose. I'm not sharing my bed with her."

Kate tested the second bed with her hand, satisfied that the mattress was hard enough. "This will do just fine."

Billy picked up the hotel telephone and requested that a cot be sent up. It seemed only fair, as he was the one who had abducted them in the first place. It would be good to show them he could be reasonable as well as threatening, sorta like the good cop/bad cop stuff he had seen on television.

Phoenix switched on the television and surfed with the remote control for a news broadcast. It didn't take her long to find what she was looking for:

The Pennsylvania state police have been alerted to keep their eyes out for a bank robber who may have fled the Washington, D.C. area where he robbed The National Trust Bank at gunpoint. Here is a video shot of the suspect. . . .

"Goddamn," said Billy, peering at the tv.

A grainy black and white shot of Billy, with spectacles, wig, and floppy mustache, appeared on the screen. The cashier was saying something and smiling at him. Then the camera swung to scan the other customers.

The announcer spoke over the video shot:

The Federal Bureau of Investigation is following up leads on the suspect. The analysis of his handwriting by the Behavioral Investigative Unit . . .

"Carmelita's grocery list," Billy smacked his head with his hand.

"Shhh." Phoenix waved at him to shut up.

. . . most likely an effeminate homosexual, over two hundred pounds, probably Hispanic with black hair, possibly into black magic, literate but emotionally unstable, likes cinema, may be a cross dresser. Could be heading anywhere but most likely toward the Miami area. If you see him, please contact the police. He's considered armed and dangerous.

Billy switched off the television. "Black magic, emotionally unstable? Where do they get these ideas?"

"The F.B.I. has a whole team of people who construct psychological profiles. What was on the grocery list?" Kate asked.

"I dunno. Beans and rice."

"Hispanic. It's a logical deduction. What else?"

"Eight black candles."

"See? Black magic." Kate had enormous faith in F.B.I. criminal profiles.

"No, Carmelita just liked the, the, the . . ."

"Color black?" Phoenix smiled.

"No. She liked the, the, the . . . surrounding of candles. That's not quite it," he said. Sometimes a specific word would hide from him, while he'd get stuck on another.

"The ambience?" Kate suggested.

"She said that black candles were mysterious and seductive."

"Are you going to tell us about her or not?" Phoenix asked.

"Why do they think I'm emotionally unstable?"

"Well, who else would rob a bank?" Phoenix rummaged through her backpack.

"Was there anything unusual about the list, anything extreme?" Kate inquired.

"Well, she put in a lot of exclamation marks after one item, because I'm always getting the wrong kind."

"That's probably it. Exclamation points show a strong emotional reaction." Kate lowered her head upon the pillow. Delicious after such a long drive.

"Yeah, but what about that 'cinema' stuff, 'literate' and all that?" Billy persisted.

Phoenix pulled out a hairbrush, lip gloss, and a pair of light pajamas. "Your Groucho Marx glasses. An' they think you're a fag 'cause it's your wife's handwriting."

"Please don't use that word, Phoenix. It's not nice. Homo-sexuals like to be called 'gay.'" Kate knew several gay men and, truth to be told, she usually enjoyed their company more than straight men. More joie de vivre.

"I don't like being called a queer," Billy groused.

"Don't be a dummy. It throws them off your track. They have you driving south, and you're headed north." *Billy needs to get himself a new set of brains*, Phoenix mused.

"Still . . ."

"They think you've got black hair because you're His-panic." Kate smiled.

"Nah, it's 'cause he wore a brown wig, and they couldn't imagine anybody would be stupid enough to wear a wig the same color as his own hair," Phoenix added.

He winced. The girl was making fun of him. But he was through making threats. "Look, I'm not going to hurt you. I told you that. But lay off the insults, will you?"

Kate angled herself off the bed, no small feat given her aching bones. She marched straight to the motel door and flung it open. She didn't want Phoenix to push him over the edge. More to the point, she had concocted a plan with alter-native options.

Plan A:

Kate addressed Phoenix. "You have a choice, young lady. Either you leave now, go out this door without another word said or you can stay. If you choose to stay, then you must make a major change in your demeanor. Stay or go, it's of no consequence to me."

Billy's mouth dropped open.

"Whaddya mean?" Phoenix got defensive.

Kate jerked her head toward the door, toward freedom, silently urging Phoenix to flee. *Go, while you have the chance, silly girl. This is the opportunity I was telling you about.* Only the girl wasn't getting the message.

Plan B then:

Kate put on her most severe expression. "In the space of less than eight hours, you've called me a 'bitch' and you've labeled Billy as 'stupid' and 'a dummy.' When either one of us says something that disagrees with you, you adopt a superior holier-than-thou attitude. Your language is vile; your grammar is atrocious; and you look like you've been sucking on lemons. There's no pleasure in being with you. Do I make myself clear?"

"But where am I going to go?" Phoenix looked at Billy.

He shrugged his shoulders. No way was he going to step into this battle. It was between them.

"That, my dear, is your problem," Kate continued. "And it is your *choice.*" Kate put a lot of emphasis on *choice*, only the girl acted deaf. *For heaven's sake, GO.* Kate tried to will that thought into Phoenix's brain.

Phoenix looked at Kate, then at her backpack crumpled on the floor. Billy wasn't going to be of any help. She was tired. The bed was comfortable. She could always change her mind tomorrow, take off, and find her own way. Even if she didn't feel all that sorry, she could fake an apology with the best of them. A necessary skill for any child. "Okay, okay. I'm sorry I said 'dummy' to you and 'bitch' to you." She swivelled her head, trying to encapsulate a two-for-one apology in a single sentence. Less painful that way.

"That's a good start," Kate said, "but there's more to it than a simple apology."

Phoenix felt her heart sink. Was Kate going to be like her mother, going on and on and on about Phoenix's behavior, clothes, choice of music? What did she have to do to get this old woman off her back?

Time for Plan C:

"I believe," Kate began, addressing them both, "that each one of us can choose how to live our lives. You can surround yourself with kindness toward others, an appreciation of beauty, and an ethic that focuses on improving the human experience. Or you can downgrade yourself into the slime of existence, foul the English language with crude vulgarities, be mean-spirited and hurtful, put yourself up by stomping down someone else, and say that the only one who has any value in this world is 'me, me, me.' That's the choice we each have, Phoenix, and it's a much more important choice than whether to leave this motel or not."

"Now take Billy for example," Kate continued.

Billy sank into the motel room chair. Some example he was. *Estupido, Bee-ly!*

"Although he has maneuvered himself into a terrible situation with the bank robbery, the abduction of you, the kidnaping of me, the stealing of Matilda . . ."

Billy felt a hole in the floor start to open up and swallow him whole. A big, black, bottomless hole.

"He has acted with restraint, even respect, toward the two of us. He hasn't hurt us. And we're beginning to slowly understand a little bit about what brought him to such a desperate act. For it's obvious to me that he's never before done such a thing." Kate smiled at him, thinking, *God, I hope this works. Sometimes you have to say a thing before it becomes true.*

Respect? Billy savored the word's sound. *Respect.* A word that let him trust himself. The black hole began to fill up with that word.

Phoenix masked an emerging smirk. Yeah, it was obvious to her that this was Billy's first effort at crime, because he certainly didn't know how to go about it.

"Desperate times call for desperate measures," Kate continued. "That's not to say I condone what he did, but I do believe, Phoenix, there is goodness in all of us, and it is our duty, as human beings, to touch the core of that goodness in each other. In short, Billy could use our help." Kate closed the door.

Amazed at this speech, Billy looked from Kate to Phoenix and back to Kate. After all that he had done to them, Kate wanted to help him?

Phoenix, too, was surprised by the turn of the lecture. Help the guy who had taken them hostage? But, in a crazy kind of way, the old lady was right. Billy was Mr. Super Klutz. He needed all the help he could get. And although she didn't appreciate the way he had dragged her into the car and threatened her with the gun, the choice was hers whether to go or to stay.

"Okay," she replied.

"Agreed then." Kate nodded, returning back to her bed. *It worked. They both think I was talking to he*r.

Billy shook his head. *Amazing how women sometimes talk a streak and then suddenly, when you're still trying to figure out what they're gabbing 'bout, they stop. Then all is calm and something's happened 'tween them and you still don't know what. But they're treating me different somehow. Sorta like the way Momma used to look at me, when I'd scrape my knees. A look brimmin' o'er with that honey peculiar to all women when they see a man stumblin' about, part pity, part lovin', part laughter—a sticky look. I don't trust it one bit. No sirree. It jus' means I've got to keep a sharper eye on them two, keep track of what they're doin'.*

Phoenix dug into her backpack and yanked out an oversized tee shirt. "Here, you can use this for a nightgown." The image of a bikini-clad singer with enormous breasts decorated the front of the shirt.

Kate frowned but accepted the offer.

"Hey," said Phoenix, "She's the best."

While Kate washed her clothes in the sink and hung them over the shower bar, Billy offered to fetch toothbrushes, combs, and toothpaste. "You come with me," he said to Phoenix, knowing that Kate wouldn't leave without her.

Kate listened at the door as their footsteps faded down the hallway. She picked up the telephone, intending to call the police, then hung up. It seemed too risky. Phoenix might get hurt in a fire fight. There had to be another way. She sat down on the bed, opened the bedside table drawer and drew out the Gideon Bible. If worse came to worse, she could always hit him on the head with it. She placed it under her pillow and waited for them to return.

"He tried to find me a charger for my iPod, but the motel didn't have one," Phoenix said, upon opening the door.

Billy rolled in a cot, then ducked momentarily into the bathroom and simply reversed his briefs. No need to wash clothes unnecessarily. He tucked the gun under the pillow, smoothed out the cot's blankets, and eased into it, ready for sleep. It had been a long, hard day.

Phoenix finally finished with her long, laborious bathroom preparations and turned off the light. She knew it would take hours for her to fall asleep, especially since her iPod was no longer working.

Kate stared at the dark ceiling, aware that Billy had fallen asleep and Phoenix had not. She could tell by their different breathing patterns. It had been a long, long time since she had slept in the same room with another person, and now there were two of them. She found it oddly comforting. The Bible, on the other hand, was hard and unforgiving. She slipped it out from under her pillow and dropped it gently to the floor.

No sooner had Billy fallen asleep, than a dream overtook him. He was standing alone on a vast plain, calling out—was it to Carmelita?—when a dust cloud swirled toward him. As the spindle of sand spiraled closer and closer, he could make out the massive presence of a buffalo herd galloping straight for him, horns lowered, a streak of animals as far as the eye could see. No place to hide.

His eyes jerked open. Disoriented, he looked around the unfamiliar motel room. The sound of tromping feet and hooves continued to rush past the window. Even Phoenix and Kate sat up straight in their beds. The illusion of a stamped-ing herd shattered with the shrieks and gleeful shouts of a million unrestrained Little Leaguers returning from a late night game.

"I hate kids, don't you?" groaned Phoenix. Her head flopped back onto the pillow.

"Ah, kids are okay. Always wanted them but . . . " He stopped there.

"But what?" Kate asked.

"Carmelita said I wasn't ready to be a father yet."

The sound of Little Leaguer feet running up and down the motel corridor didn't diminish one iota. It would be a long time before any of them would find sleep.

"So tell us about her." Phoenix clasped her hands behind her head, studying the dark ceiling.

"I dunno. What can I say? Carmelita's beautiful. Got eyes that do magic on you, know what I mean? Like they turn color, draw you in. Built like a goddess an' she cooks like one too. Happiest day of my life when she agreed to marry me." He sighed.

There was nothing Billy enjoyed more than talking about or thinking about his beloved Carmelita.

"I jus' couldn't believe it, that somebody like that would marry somebody like me. Not that I'm bad looking or nuthin', but you've got to see Carmelita to know what I mean. All the guys at the plant were jealous. They told me she was jus' marrying me to become a U.S. citizen, but I know different. She loves me. They were jus' saying that 'cuz they wanted her to choose one of them." Billy chuckled.

"What went wrong?" Kate asked.

"The plant closed down. 'Outsourcing,' they called it. Sent my job to Mexico. I tried but couldn't find another job. Carmelita told me that I hadda move out, until I could make some money. Weren't her fault."

"Wasn't," Kate said.

"Well, it wasn't, all I'm saying." Billy was anxious that they not criticize his wife.

Phoenix coughed, trying to clear the scorn from her voice. "Why didn't she get a job?"

"'Cuz she's going to school to get an education. I . . . I'm not bright 'nuf to do that. I can't hardly expect her to go to college and work too. But my unemployment check barely covers her tuition, as it is."

"Well, that's very thoughtful of you, Billy, to try to take care of your wife that way," Kate said.

What a wus. Phoenix rolled her eyes.

"Carmelita thought it best for me to leave our apartment until I can find a job, but there's jus' no jobs around."

"And so you decided to rob the bank?" Kate's voice was kind, gentle, and understanding.

"I know it's wrong, but I thought jus' this once. I was desperate to see her." He faltered in the telling of it.

"And?" Kate encouraged him to continue.

Tears welled in his eyes. He was glad the room was dark. He began to choke on the words. "There . . . there were some others coming to the apartment, to . . . to see her an'. . . ." He couldn't finish.

"No," said Kate, shocked.

"Other guys were shagging your wife?" Phoenix asked. *Unbelievable.*

"You don't understand," he said. "She's so beautiful. Like an angel."

His defense of Carmelita met with complete silence.

Phoenix shifted in Kate's direction. "You know what you said earlier?"

"Yes," Kate answered.

"I see whatcha mean," Phoenix said.

The next morning, it was agreed that Billy would do most of the driving. Shadowing both females, he allowed Kate to pick up some necessary traveling clothes and an overnight bag at a shopping center. At each store, Kate told the sales-people that he'd pay the bill. He hoped she wouldn't exhaust his diminishing pile of cash.

Afterwards, Matilda headed north toward Rochester. "We'll turn west soon, won't we?" Phoenix asked.

Sitting in the front seat, Kate traced the map route with her finger. "Don't worry, dear. You have to head northward for Seattle as well."

"I bet your Dad's worried about you." Billy could imagine the terror he'd feel if he had a daughter who'd suddenly van-ished into nowhere. It made him feel guilty for what he had done, snatching the poor kid off the street.

"I'm sure he's out nailing my picture on every corner."

Kate looked at her with a jaundiced eye.

"A really good Dad, huh?" Billy believed that most fami-lies had wonderful fathers that spent hours and hours of devoted time with their children. The kind of father he had seen on television, although that hadn't been his experience. He had never known his dad.

"The greatest." Phoenix nodded her head.

"Does he know you're coming?" asked Kate.

"Well, sort of. He'd want me to come if I asked him."

"Of course he would," chorused Billy.

"Did you ever think of preparing him for your arrival?" Kate probed.

"Well, his friend, Talia, didn't really want me around. And I overheard Mom on the phone say to someone that Dad and

Talia were probably splitting up. So I thought this was a good time."

"Your parents ain't married?" Billy was confused.

"No," answered Phoenix.

"Aren't," inserted Kate.

"Aren't," repeated Billy.

"No, they never got married. But he's still my Dad and he's a great dad, and he's going to be real happy when he opens the door and finds me standing there."

"Of course he will," said Billy. He could see it now. Phoenix's father swooping her up in his strong arms, full of joy on seeing her.

"He'll be quite surprised, I'm sure," Kate added.

Neither one of them caught the irony of her remark.

F O U R

N E W   Y O R K

$\mathcal{M}$atilda cruised along, as if it were everyday she got to drive long distances. Kate was really quite proud of her, and Billy's obvious admiration for Matilda had been the first clue to the potential goodness of his character. She handled the interstate highways like an old pro, not giving ground to the decked-out vans, the racy Porsche or two, and the ubiquitous SUVs that hogged the road and blocked the view.

When they reached the city limits of Rochester, Phoenix insisted that they all get out of the car for that special "Kodak moment." She stopped a jogger in mid-stride and pressed her camera upon him. "Would you take a picture of us in front of the city limits sign? That'll prove to my friends that I'm not making all this up. Come on, Kate. you got to be in the picture too."

Kate reluctantly moved into the frame wondering, *Should I put on a terrified face to show I'm a hostage, not an accomplice?*

But the jogger sang out, "Cheese!" and Kate broke into a smile.

Billy then asked the jogger to take a picture of them standing next to Matilda. He rested his right hand on the old car's left flank and looped his right arm through Kate's arm. Phoenix crouched down in front of them. "A family photo," he said.

They climbed back into Matilda and headed west on Lake Ontario State Parkway, edging the Great Lake. "Jimminee Cricket," Billy exclaimed, "That can't be no lake. It's gotta be the ocean."

"In grammar, that's known as a double negative, Billy," Kate said.

Billy looked puzzled.

Phoenix explained, "Two no's equal one yes."

Kate added, "If you say 'that can't be a lake,' then we know it must be something other than a lake. It's the same thing if you say 'that be no lake,' although that sounds like dialect. But when you say 'no' twice, then your second 'no' contradicts your first 'no.' Now do you understand?"

"My momma didn't teach me no grammar or nuthin' like that," Billy answered.

"Lost cause," Phoenix whispered.

Kate tapped Billy on the arm. "You do just fine, Billy."

Phoenix began to shift restlessly in the back seat. "So if we aren't going to listen to the car radio, and there's no tape deck, and I need an iPod charger, what am I supposed to do? Talk about current events, car mechanics, or proper el-o-cu-tion with the two of you?" A tone of voice that wavered between a screech and a whine.

"Meditate. Daydream. Compose a poem. Watch the lake scenery. Tell us a story." Kate was full of suggestions. The younger generation appalled her with their demands for instant, passive entertainment, a need to fill each and every moment with sensory stimulation.

"Daydreaming and story telling is for babies," Phoenix said. "I'm *warning* you. I'm teetering on the edge of profanity. My mind is shrinking by the minute."

"I can't stand her fussing. Can't you do anything?" Billy addressed Kate. "You're a woman."

A total non sequitur, thought Kate. *What does being a woman have to do with satisfying the needs of a teenager for constant excitement?* But then a notion struck her. She reached into her pocketbook and pulled out a paperback novel, entitled *Double Trouble*. "Try this." She handed it back over the seat to Phoenix.

Phoenix studied the book's cover: a bare-chested man of rippling muscles was embracing a woman with long, blond, tumbling hair, bent over backwards in the man's powerful arms. In the background, a frothy surf assaulted an ocean beach. The handsome dude was staring down into the woman's mammoth breasts, which were about to spill out of her partially unbuttoned blouse.

"What's this?"

"A romance novel. Haven't you ever read one?" Kate adored romance novels. Especially in the wee hours of the night when she was experiencing insomnia.

"I'm an Aquarian. I read the astrology section in the newspaper every day. The astrologer says I wobble between insanity and genius. Books are too slow, you know?"

Kate could hardly believe her ears. Not to know the joy of reading, of lingering over well-stated phrases, tightly constructed plots, tear-jerking metaphors. "What about you, Billy? You read, don't you?"

"Sports page, sometimes a comic book or two." Billy didn't want either one of them to know that he found it difficult to read. Always had.

Well, thought Kate, *it's never to late to learn. "Double Trouble* is hot off the press, and the author enjoys an excellent reputation."

Phoenix examined the cover some more. Why would any woman let a man contort her backwards into such a torturous embrace? "Fel-i-ci-ty Dare." She enunciated the author's name. "What kind of name is that?"

Kate could feel her spine stiffening. "Why it's a good name. A pseudonym, most likely."

"A what?" asked Billy.

"A fake name," Phoenix answered. "A stupid name if you ask me. The author probably didn't want others to know she writes this kind of book."

"What kind of book do you think it is?" Kate hated when people leapt to premature conclusions.

Phoenix didn't really know. She shrugged her shoulders.

"Precisely," said Kate. "Why don't you first read the book and then bestow your critique upon it."

"Hey," suggested Billy, "I'd kinda like to hear it. It'd pass the time. Would'cha read it out loud?"

Reading a dumb book aloud was certainly better than sitting in the car twiddling her thumbs and picking her nose. Phoenix cracked open the book and cleared her throat.

DOUBLE TROUBLE
by Felicity Dare

Day One

A cold North Shore wind tore at her thin dress and second-hand coat, as Daisy Hill once more scanned the Boston Globe advertisement for a nanny's position. "Wanted: a woman with child care experience, preferably with a knowledge of foreign languages." The only foreign words Daisy knew were curse words, taught to her by traveling sailors who had drifted into Joe's Diner one day. Still, when she had telephoned, Mrs. Catherine DuMaurier had seemed interested in interviewing her for the position. Three subway switches and two bus transfers transported her to the North Shore suburb where the DuMaurier family resided.

This may be the biggest mistake in my life, Daisy mused. The large brick facade prefaced by a row of daunting white pillars, the manicured lawn dotted with sculpted flower beds, and the long curling driveway through two rows of neatly pruned trees displayed a wealth far beyond Daisy's experience.

"Holy Moly," she exclaimed. But then she reminded herself that it was luck that had encouraged her to come, luck which gave her the courage to leave Joe's Diner. It took only a single night out with the other waitresses at a Chinese restaurant and a fortune cookie that read, "Go north, young man. Blessed fortune awaits you."

Despite all the hardships in her life, Daisy believed in luck. The fortune cookie was an omen of good things to come. That very night she had packed her bags, given notice to the lecherous Joe, and quit the North Carolina tidewater country, heading all the way to Boston, Massachusetts where her fortune awaited her.

Before treasure hunting, she had to find a job. Although only twenty-six-years old, she had done just about every kind of work imaginable: crab picking, dog clipping, elder care with Alzheimer folk, exercising horses and cleaning stables, trail maintenance for a state park, baby sitting and, of course, waitressing at Joe's Diner. Being a nanny couldn't be much worse than mucking stalls, she figured.

Smoothing down the wrinkles in her only dress, Daisy took a deep breath and started walking down the long driveway to the DuMaurier residence. She concentrated on counting the number of visible windows: "One, two, four . . . twelve."

"Your hair is different, Missus. Very pretty that way," a male voice interrupted.

Daisy jumped, startled. Off to the side, an elderly man in a tweed gardener's cap nodded to her. He was leaning against the shovel, where he'd been turning over the flower bed.

She gave him a smile and replied, "Why thank you, Suh. Ah do appreciate you saying that."

He looked confused by her southern accent. Daisy sighed. She was now in the North, and she might as well get used to talking the Yankee way. She pursed her lips together, tightened her jaw muscles, and tried to scissor her words. "Excuse me," she mouthed, not knowing if he heard it or not. She turned and headed toward the house.

"I parked my car in Harvard yard. I paacked my cah in Haavaad yaad. I perked my curr in Harrverd yurd." She rolled the words on her tongue, trying every which way to approximate the Bostonian accent, but nothing seemed to sound right.

The massive front door sported a huge brass ring hanging down from the nose of a lion, frozen in mid-roar. Daisy looked around for a buzzer but couldn't find any. She grabbed the brass ring and clocked it against the door. Before she could rap a second time, the door swung open. Standing there, dressed out in a spiffy tie and jacket, was a black man.

"Mr. DuMaurier?" she inquired. Had to be the richest black folk she'd ever seen.

"He's not in right now. May I help you?" The man smiled, studying her face. "Are you perhaps a relative of the DuMauriers?"

"No," she answered most emphatically.

"Well then, would you like to leave a card?"

The jack of hearts leapt to her mind, then she realized he meant a card of a different sort. "I'm here for an interview for the nanny's job."

"Oh, I see. Next time, please use the side door. That's for the employees."

Daisy couldn't help noticing the "s" after the word employee.

The butler led her into a large room paneled with the glossiest mahogany wood that Daisy had ever seen. He once more gave her a curious look, then disappeared down the long hallway in search of Mrs. DuMaurier.

Daisy moseyed around the room, trailing her fingers over the shiny wood sills of large windows overlooking a rose garden and fountain. Bookcases, filled to the top with leather-bound volumes, dominated the room. Hands behind her back, she moved from one case to another, devouring the titles but not daring to touch the books. History, philosophy, and something called The Great Classics occupied most of the space.

"Uh hum," interrupted the butler. "This is the woman you wanted to interview, Mrs. DuMaurier. He stepped to the side, letting Catherine DuMaurier sweep into the library.

"Thank you," she said to the butler, "You may go now, Edward." He closed the door behind him.

Catherine and Daisy stood facing each other, staring at each other, not saying a word. No polite introductions or hand shakes. Catherine wiped her brow, as if to dispel a hallucination. Daisy blinked three times, wondering if she had somehow overslept and was now snared in a dream. The two women could not believe their own eyes.

It was as if each one of them was standing alone in the room, peering into a mirror, facing their own reflections. So alike were the facial features, the width and height of their slender figures, that the two of them could easily be mistaken for the other. Only the color and style of hair set them apart. Daisy's hair was chestnut brown, cut short and easy to fix. Long, shiny blond locks cascaded down Catherine's back, luxuriant and sensual.

Catherine found herself at a loss for words, "You are . . ."

"Daisy, ma'am. Daisy Hill." Daisy extended her hand.

Catherine's hand, nails manicured and glossed to perfection, returned a gentle shake.

"I came about the nanny's job." Daisy raised the advertisement in her hand. She noted a distracted look in Mrs. DuMaurier's eyes. Quickly Daisy summarized her work history, then asked about the children, aware that Mrs. DuMaurier continued to stare at her. Down South, that was considered rude, but Daisy didn't yet know the Yankee customs.

"The children? Oh, yes. There's Anthony who's four and Charlotte who is in the terrible twos. Anthony is a bit of a handful, and Charlotte doesn't like to be told 'no.' Do you have any children?"

Catherine's mind was elsewhere. She knew she sounded preoccupied, but she wanted to know more about this woman who looked so much like her.

"No, ma'am. Never been married."

Catherine could see that the hazel color of Daisy's eyes was a shade different than her own deep blue, but that could be corrected by contact lenses. "Do you wear glasses?"

Daisy appeared embarrassed. "Yes. I've got them in my bag here, but I thought I'd look better for the interview without 'em.'"

"Ah," Catherine sighed with relief. That, at least, would offer no problem.

"Why?" asked Daisy. Maybe the woman didn't like people with glasses.

"Well, I have a proposition for you."

"A proposition?" Daisy knew that something different was about to happen. She had a second sense for that kind of thing.

"I think you could be of more use to me than simply as a nanny." Catherine circled around Daisy, studying her from every angle.

Daisy didn't like it one bit. Maybe she ought to gather up her bag and leave. She wasn't going to stand for any kind of beauty contest.

"You're perfect, Miss Hill. Why I couldn't have found anyone better."

Daisy stepped back a couple of steps.

"Excuse me, you must be terribly confused. Do sit down." Catherine's voice was solicitous. "Let me explain."

Daisy perched on the edge of the chair, ready to flee if need be. But she had to admit she was a mite curious.

Catherine positioned herself opposite of Daisy. She reached out to a nearby table and picked up a shiny silver box, which she opened and pulled out a cigarette. "Do you . . ."

Daisy shook her head.

"Most sensible of you to be sure." Catherine lit the cigarette and sat back on the couch. "It can't be beyond your notice, that you and I are spitting images of each other, except for our hair and the color of our eyes. I have never in my life encountered someone so much like a reflection of myself."

Daisy nodded, not sure where Catherine was going in this conversation.

"Sometimes life presents one with extraordinary opportunities, and one would be an utter fool to ignore those moments." She exhaled an elegant line of smoke in the air.

She continued, "Before I married Paul and had the children, I was quite famous as a photographer with a social conscience. Typically, I'd shoot a peaceful, natural landscape, such as a sunset over the ocean, a wildflower meadow, a misty old-growth forest. Then I would make a double exposure, inserting shots of man-made violence and the agony of the innocents, those the world coldly calls 'collateral damage.' Here. Take a look at this one."

She removed a framed photograph from the wall and handed it to Daisy. In the lush green jungle background, a waterfall gushed from the eyes of a refugee woman holding her dead baby. "It's accurate to say that I was making a political and aesthetic statement. I call my technique 'double refraction,' because my intent is to cast a different light onto people's perceptions."

Daisy had to admit to herself that it was a jarring, disturbing image. She handed it back to Catherine, not wanting to look at it longer than was polite.

Catherine rehung it on the wall. "I took that photo in Africa before I had children. But since the children, I've been limited in my ability to go where the action is. I tried to make do, using only shots of individual violence in this country, but it's not been successful. People are beginning to forget my work. I need to go to the world's

current war zones, capture the suffering on a mass scale. It's important work, but it's a project that requires a year of travel and being
away from the family."

Catherine sat down, smoothed out her skirt with nervous hands,
and picked up her cigarette. "You must consider me a terrible mother
for even contemplating such a plan."

Before Daisy could even think of an appropriate response,
Catherine added, "Of course, this idea would be totally unaccept-
able to Paul. The condemnation and guilt I'd experience from family
and friends for choosing to follow my vision would make my life miserable. So, I've been trapped. Until now, that is."

Daisy still didn't get the picture.

"It's not like we have the best of marriages, you understand. Paul
tries to be a good husband, but he expects me to love being a
mother and to be happy simply being his wife." She blew smoke rings
in the air. "And although I dearly love the children, I am neither a
happy mother nor a good wife."

Catherine stole a peek to see how Daisy was receiving this confession, but the woman in front of her gave no reaction. Catherine
pressed on. "The truth is that not only do I feel trapped by the children, but I no longer love my husband. An impossible situation
really. And then you arrive. I am beginning to see a way out of my
predicament. Something that will meet my needs, the children's
needs and benefit you handsomely."

"How's that?" Daisy was curious.

"You want to earn money. I want to travel, do my photography.
So, if you would be willing to take my place for one year, not only
will I pay you a generous monthly stipend, but at the end of the year,
I will give you a bonus of two hundred thousand dollars. "

Daisy blinked. "Two hundred thousand dollars?" The amount
staggered the imagination.

"A fifth of a million dollars." Catherine smiled. The bait dangled, the hook was setting.

"But the hair, the eyes," Daisy protested.

"I'll get my hair cut, and you will get yours dyed blond. We'll purchase contact lenses, similar to my own, that will color your eyes a blue to match mine."

Daisy swallowed. It was an outrageous idea, of course. Totally unworkable. But two hundred thousand dollars was an awful lot of smackers.

"That way," Catherine continued, "nobody needs be any the wiser. Paul won't condemn me, and the children won't feel abandoned. I'll find you an apartment in the next town. Over the next month, you and I will secretly meet everyday. I will tutor you in everything, what each one of them is like, how to manage the household account and the staff, the use of my signature stamp for checks. Everything. I am a very thorough woman.

"But won't the children see the difference?"

"Children at their age only notice themselves. Believe me, you'll do just fine." Catherine decided that now was not the time to confess that the children were much closer to their father than to her.

"Yes, but what about your husband? Won't he expect . . ." Daisy felt embarrassed to bring up the subject.

"Sex? No, you needn't worry about that. Anthony was a spermicide condom baby and Charlotte a birth-control pill baby. I told him, 'no more children.' But Paul refuses to get a vasectomy, so there you are. We haven't been together since the birth of Charlotte. We sleep in separate bedrooms. It's preferable that way."

"But surely, he'll be able to sense that I'm not you."

Catherine laughed with an undertone of bitterness. "He won't, I tell you. The man is too busy working. Between his hours on the job and his time with the children, there have been precious few moments for just the two of us. Now, this is my plan. I'll go ahead and find somebody else to fill the nanny's position. You and I will spend a month smoothing over our considerable differences. Then, when I decide that you're ready, you'll step into my place and take on my identity as Catherine DuMaurier. Daisy Hill will simply disappear for the next year. And as long as you make sure the house is running to order and that the children are being adequately supervised, you can spend the time as me any which way you choose. You can go to school for all I care. The only thing I require is that you tell nobody about our secret. Are you willing to do it?" She stubbed out her cigarette.

Daisy sat a long time, looking out the window to the rose garden and the fountain spouting diamond-speckled water into the air. What would it be like to live in such luxury? To own a pot of gold in only one year's time? She could buy land, a house, a brand new car. She could travel and see the whole United States. She could even go to college, while playing the high and mighty Mrs. DuMaurier.

A part of her argued, *this is all wrong. Who do you think you are anyway, to be able to carry it off?* But Daisy had never shrank from anything for fear of being made the fool. She had always been curious about other people's lives. Here was her great chance to step out of her own humdrum existence and step into someone's else's life, so different from her own. Nor did she have any family who would worry about her disappearance.

Go on, do it. What do you have to lose? It was true that the resemblance between the two of them was uncanny. Daisy finally nodded. "Okay, I'm willing."

Catherine gleefully clapped her hands and headed for the study door. "What fun it will be to transform you. Let me make the calls immediately to get you situated in an apartment. Over this next month, you and I are going to work miracles."

Phoenix slapped the book shut. "Sure, like the husband isn't going to know that his wife is really someone else? What a stupid story."

"I kind of like it," Billy said. "I want to know what happens next."

"Catherine is going to coach Daisy on all the family members," Kate rejoined. Looking back at Phoenix, she asked, "If you were a DuMaurier, how would Catherine describe you?"

"I don't know, but I'd know for sure if somebody else pretended to be my mother."

"It's an interesting story line," Kate continued. "Obviously the author is setting the stage for all kinds of trouble, don't you think?"

Billy added, "I like the way the chapter ended, you know. It makes you want to read more."

Phoenix knew he was hinting. "I'm tired of reading. I'm getting hoarse."

"Do you know why chapters always have that hook at the end?" asked Kate.

Billy shook his head.

"Well, Charles Dickens invented the modern form of the novel. He wrote his books in serial form for the newspaper, so each chapter corresponded to that day's section of his book. Many people bought the newspapers simply to read the next installment."

Looking out the car window, Phoenix grumbled, "Catherine DuMaurier doesn't seem to care much about what happens to her children."

"No, she doesn't," Kate said.

As Matilda headed along the Lake Ontario shoreline, signs for *The Falls* cropped up along the road.

"I've never been to Niagara Falls in my whole life," Phoenix said in her most pitiful voice.

"If it's Canada where you're headed, we can cross over there," Kate suggested.

"Please, please, pretty please." It was the teenager's super polite voice.

"Okay," Billy replied, "Niagra, here we come."

No sooner did they arrive at the upper part of the Falls to eat lunch than Phoenix began a campaign to take the boat trip to the base of the Falls. "Please, please, please, oh pretty, pretty please." It was enough to drive any adult completely bonkers.

So they said yes, boarded the boat, and rode to the thunderous Falls, only to be drenched by the spray of turbulent white water. In the sparkling afternoon haze, Phoenix alternated between gazing at the awesome pull of the Falls to scanning the boat crowd for young teenage males, most of whom she found either too pimpled or scrawny.

Kate fantasized about the danger of barreling over the tremendous height. What kind of death-defying courage and foolishness would it take? Why would anyone do such a silly stunt?

Billy, too, was fascinated by the cascading waters, concluding that only natural violence could have split one continent into two countries.

All three returned to Matilda, damp but refreshed. "Well, we won't have to take a shower tonight, that's for sure." Billy shook the water out of his hair.

Phoenix excused herself for a moment and came back, loaded with soft pretzels, mustard, and sodas for each of them. "Thank you for a wonderful afternoon." She knew how important it is to reward adults for good behavior.

Billy bit into the large, doughy pretzel, enjoying the sudden snap of salt upon the tongue. Leaning against Matilda, he chewed and mumbled, "I've always wanted to see the States. You know, jus' get into a car and drive. That's my idea of a vacation. But . . ."

Both Kate and Phoenix anticipated that Carmelita was about to impose herself.

"Carmelita, she didn't like much to travel. Said it was boring. She'd rather go someplace to shop. When we did go to some of the sights, she'd sit in the car, tell me she could see everything just fine from there."

He smiled. "Now here I am 'bout to enter into a different country. Imagine that. Say, do we need passports or anything?" It suddenly occurred to him that maybe Canada would refuse them admission.

Kate shook her head.

Phoenix piped up, "Peut-etre je dois parler francais?"

"Huh?" Billy was confused.

"Non, ici ce n'est pas necessaire," Kate replied. "So you know how to speak French?"

"Oh," Billy grunted.

"Yeah." Phoenix bit into the last section of her pretzel.

Kate turned toward Billy. "Part of Canada, the province of Quebec, speaks French whereas most of Canada speaks English. The part we'll be entering is English speaking."

"That's a relief," he said, dusting off the crumbs, spitting onto the ground, and climbing into the driver's seat. "Let's get outta here."

"Let's blow this joint," echoed Phoenix.

Made up of sun, spray, warm pretzels, the roar of the Falls, and a grand sense of adventure, a giddy feeling pervaded the group. The tension of their earlier fear had dissipated. More like a group of tourists than hostages with a desperado.

Kate looked at the map and directed Billy toward Canada. "Westward ho," she shouted, surprised at her own exuberance.

FIVE

CANADA

Phoenix expected Canada to look like Switzerland, snow-capped mountains and lush, green valleys. Instead, small grey towns and flat, brown landscapes greeted her.

"You're thinking of the Canadian Rockies," Kate said. "This area of Canada is mostly farming."

The bliss of their Niagara Falls adventure soon wore off. It wasn't long before Phoenix once again began to chafe in the company of two adults.

"This is fucking pathetic," she complained. "Why can't you stop and let me get an iPod charger? I'll even pay for it with my own money."

"I won't allow such language in my car," Kate said.

"Why don't you chill out?" She lowered her eyes into the meanest, orneriest look she could muster. "I'm tired of you always correcting *my* words and *his* grammar."

Kate frowned. "Then, you tell me, what does sexual intercourse have to do with your inability to withstand a delay in gratification?"

Phoenix bunched her arms together and refused to answer.

"Your generation applies the words 'fuck,' 'fucking,' 'mother-fucking' to anything that causes them the briefest of irritations. Now I'm most curious. What is it about the sexual act that is so full of anger for you young people?"

Phoenix knew that Kate didn't get it, that "fuck" was simply the fastest way to rile the older folk.

Kate continued, "I challenge you for one day only, every time you use the word "fuck," replace it with 'intercourse.' See how that sounds when you return the word back to its original meaning."

"This is mother-fucking pathetic," Phoenix muttered.

"Try 'maternal-intercoursing pathetic,'" Kate answered.

Phoenix lowered her eyes, demonstrating that she was not the least bit amused. "Stop!" she shouted.

Billy's foot slammed down on the brakes before he realized Phoenix's outburst was not a command directed at him. "Jeez," he complained, "don't do that to me. You almost gave me a heart attack." To make things worse, Matilda choked down and needed coaxing to get back up to speed. They began to swing westward, leaving the Lake Ontario shoreline.

"I said Stop," Phoenix screeched.

Billy pulled the car over to the breakdown lane. "What's your problem?"

"I can't ride anymore with her in the same car."

"My car," Kate reminded her.

"Tough shit," Phoenix retorted. "You have to do what Billy says. He's the one driving it."

Both females turned to stare at him. Billy dropped his head upon the wheel, as if his brain was hurting him. "Can't you two find a way to get along?"

"No way," answered Phoenix.

"I simply won't allow bad language in this car." That was all Kate had to say about the matter.

Billy raised his head and wearily sighed, "Okay." He pulled Matilda off the first exit, drove down a country road for about a quarter of a mile and stopped the car. He reached over Kate's lap, yanked open the front passenger door, and said, "You can get out now."

"Yes," exclaimed Phoenix.

Kate looked bewildered. Stretching in front of her and to both sides of the road were nothing but wheat fields. She didn't budge.

"You too." Billy turned around toward the teenager in the back seat. "Out of the car."

"What the ff . . . ?" Phoenix cut off the swear word in mid-voice.

Kate didn't move. "It's my car." She spoke slowly and with as much authority as she could invoke.

"Yes, it is," agreed Billy, "but it's my head, an' I can't take any more of this cat-fighting 'tween the two of you. We had a nice time at The Falls, but all you've been doin' since we left the States is hiss and scratch at one 'nuther, an' I've had it up to here." He slapped the bottom side of his chin. "So, get out of the car an' let me drive away in peace. Besides feeding the two of you is goin' to eat up all my money 'til I have none left."

Phoenix's eyes began to tear up. "But where can I go? You can't leave me stranded in a foreign land."

"I'm not going anywhere either. Besides," Kate added. "I'm just beginning to have fun."

Fun? Billy's jaw dropped.

"I'm giving you your freedom, don't you understand?" He didn't need hostages any longer.

"Well, that's just too bad, Billy, because we're not leaving this car. Isn't that right, Phoenix?" Kate pulled the car door shut.

Phoenix nodded.

"I think we can come to some agreement here." Kate pushed down the door lock. "There will be no more nasty words. Phoenix will clean up her language. I will try not to sound like an English school marm. And we will all treat each other with respect. Agreed?"

Phoenix gave a reluctant nod. Kate sat back, convinced she had settled the matter, and that they could now proceed with their journey.

"But I'm gonna run outta money soon." To Billy, that was the most pathetic statement of all. What had the bank robbery been all about in the first place? He slumped his head once again upon the wheel of the car. To the amazement of his two passengers, his shoulders began to tremble.

How easily a man slips from anger into sadness, thought Kate. She placed a comforting hand upon his right shoulder.

I don't get it, thought Phoenix. *First, he wants to throw us out of the car, and now he's crying like a baby.*

"I have a credit card which we can use," Kate said.

Billy shielded his face from their view.

Phoenix suddenly understood. "I've got some money too . . . well a little bit of money. I'd be willing to share some of it."

"So you see, Billy, not all is lost. Sometimes we have to do a bit of wandering before we can truly find our way home." A little bit of folk wisdom was often useful in times like these, as long as it was uplifting in tone.

Billy's ragged breathing calmed down. He had to admit that he enjoyed being comforted. Nor was he beyond leaning a bit more on their warm, maternal sympathies. "I'd like it if you could read in that book while I'm driving. Helps keep my mind offa my troubles."

"Of course we can. Phoenix, would you like me to take the next section or would you rather do it?"

Although tired from a full day and beginning to feel the hunger of late afternoon, Phoenix would have stood on her head if that was required to keep Billy happy and driving her westward. "Okay," she replied, pulling out the paperback novel.

Day Thirty

Over the following month, Catherine and Daisy met every day at that apartment. Not only did they work on removing any trace of Daisy's southern accent, but Catherine taught her fine etiquette and manners. A professional hair dresser snipped off Catherine's luxurious locks into a stylish cut that highlighted her long and delicate neck. Daisy's hair was shaped accordingly and dyed to the same color blond. Together they shopped for contact lenses that tinted Daisy's eyes a deep sea blue color. As their weight and shapes were nearly identical, no extra adjustments were needed in that department.

Catherine coached Daisy about money matters and staff management. "If you have any difficulty finding something, ask Serena. She's been with me forever. In fact, Serena was there the day I was born and came to work for me after my parents died. I pay her well. She's the only staff person for whom we have provided an apartment in our house. She knows everything, although I haven't told her about our little secret."

Catherine beamed with pleasure. Something about having a secret was absolutely delicious to her. All her life, she had had to bend herself to the whims of others around her, and now she was about to taste freedom, do what *she* wanted to do.

"Now, let me tell you about the children. Anthony is four and currently going through a stage when he doesn't particularly like women. In fact, the last nanny left in a huff after Anthony kicked her in the shins. Paul worries that our son might be 'hyperactive,' but I think his tantrums are reinforced by his father's overindulgent behavior. Since Paul works all the time, disciplining the children has naturally fallen into my lap. If Paul would only be more consistent . . ." Catherine shook her head. "Perhaps you'll have some good ideas on how to handle him. Anthony, that is."

Daisy noted that Catherine hadn't brought up any of these difficulties earlier in their conversations. *Probably didn't want to scare me off.*

"Two-year-old Charlotte is a doll, pretty as a picture. She reminds me of myself when I was her age. She's easy to get along with, except at bedtime. Then there is always a struggle." Catherine sighed. "I will really miss them."

"Tell me about your husband," interrupted Daisy. She felt confident in her abilities to handle the children. It was Mr. DuMaurier who worried her the most. Daisy had only had two brief relationships with men so her knowledge of them was far more limited than her expertise in demented old folk, Shetland Sheepdogs, and quarter horses.

"He's very handsome." Catherine studied Daisy's reactions with amusement. "He's six feet two inches, thirty-six years old, an Ivy League graduate of the University of Pennsylvania with a double major in human relations and computers. People have described him as 'ambitious,' probably because he is a genius at figuring out what people want and finding a way to meet that need, while making a lot of money in the process. I am one of the few people who baffle Paul, because he hasn't the slightest idea what it is that I truly want. Perhaps, that's what intrigued him about me in the first place."

"What does he do for a living?" Daisy didn't know if she'd feel comfortable living with someone who could see right through you. She'd made a life-long habit of keeping her own thoughts to herself. Safer that way.

"Well, when Paul was in his twenties, he discovered that single people in rural areas have a difficult time meeting other single people with similar values, especially if they didn't want to bar-hop or join a church group. So he set up and franchised *The Right Connection* with self-administered personality tests, so that people could get to know like-minded individuals through a computer dating network. The business took off like wildfire. Then he developed computerized software tests which produce a decision-making profile for business people. That venture has also proved hugely successful. Of course, it takes a lot of time and energy to keep up the franchise business, while creating new ways that psychology and computers can interface in a profitable manner. He works all the time."

Catherine stopped to see how well Daisy was digesting all this information. She could think of nothing more boring than to talk of Paul's projects.

"Ever since Charlotte's birth, Paul has periodically indulged in drinking too much. He's not an alcoholic, nor does he become abusive when he drinks. I don't approve, nonetheless. It's boorish behavior. There was a time in my life when I thought there was not a better looking, more stimulating man in the whole world than my husband. But he's . . ." Catherine searched for the right description. "He's lost the capacity for having fun, for celebrating life. He's become far too serious. Perhaps it's the responsibility of having two children or a business that has expanded too rapidly. I don't know." Catherine's hands fluttered in the air, dismissing the obvious explanation.

Perhaps, he's simply horny for his wife, Daisy thought.

Conversations and daily lessons such as these finally convinced Catherine that Daisy was as ready as she could be. She knew there would be some slippage, but she guessed that Paul would be too busy and the children too self-occupied to notice. Serena, the black housekeeper, was another matter. Catherine prepped Serena by complaining that her hormones were getting her all mixed up and "that I'm just not myself anymore." Serena was a great believer in hormonal destiny.

Departure day finally arrived. Catherine found herself fawning over the children, kissing them twice over, as they headed off to a play date with other children. She went into their bedrooms, smoothed their covers, and left a note under each one's pillow. REMEMBER, I LOVE YOU. MOMMY. She tucked recent photographs of them in her wallet, wanting to linger but needing to hurry before Serena returned from grocery shopping.

Catherine secretly packed her bags, leaving most of her clothes in the closet and taking only the bare necessities. She dropped the bags into the car, drove over to Daisy's apartment, slipped into different clothing, and gave Daisy the keys. While Catherine called for a taxi, Daisy tried on Catherine's dress. It fit perfectly. Just before leaving the apartment, Catherine turned around and said, "Good luck. I'll try to contact you when I can, but that won't be often as I'm off to Africa. I'm doing the right thing, aren't I? Of course I am. Of course I am. Oh, I almost forgot. Here, take this." Nervously, Catherine slipped off her braided gold wedding band and placed it on Daisy's finger.

"The children will be home at two o'clock and Paul at six o'clock. Serena will be expecting that I, I mean *you*, will be there in another hour or so. Any last questions?"

Daisy couldn't think of any. Catherine had been incredibly thorough in her coaching, although it made her nervous that there was no way for her to contact Catherine if the need should arise. Catherine seemed to have a great deal of faith that Paul could handle any emergency, as long as he didn't know about the switch.

"I will see you at this time next year." As fast as a flashbulb, Catherine whisked out of the apartment, camera equipment in tow. Down on the street, a taxi waited for her.

Daisy closed up the apartment, having already sent her last postcards to her friends at Joe's Diner. She was dying to tell them about her latest escapade, but Catherine had sworn her to absolute secrecy. Daisy climbed into Catherine's cream-colored, leather-upholstered BMW and drove ever so carefully toward the DuMaurier residence. Despite the temptation, she didn't gun the accelerator even once. Over and over, she recited the separate names of the household staff.

"Missus." The gardener tipped his hat, as she turned into the long driveway.

"Good morning, John." She smiled, enunciating her words in the northern tradition.

Once inside the house, Daisy found her way to Catherine's bedroom, climbing up the sweeping stairway, rubbing her hand along the glossy, mahogany railing. In the bedroom, the plump, elderly Serena was making the bed and straightening the room.

"What will you be wanting for lunch, Sweetpea?" Serena's southern drawl immediately warmed its way into Daisy's heart.

"Oh, I'll take a look in the 'fridge for myself."

Serena shot her a puzzled look.

"Whatever is easiest for you," amended Daisy. *This was not going to be as easy as Mrs. DuMaurier guessed.*

Serena gave her a sideways glance, then left the room without saying another word.

Daisy arranged things to her liking, amazed at all the different kinds of make-up on the bureau top. Carefully, she gathered up the lipsticks, eye colors, blush powders and stacked them in an empty reed basket, and from her pocketbook pulled out her one favorite brand of lipstick and her one eyebrow pencil. *That's all any woman needs.*

When she descended at noon, lunch was already set out on the table. Daisy seated herself and proceeded to examine the four quarters of a crustless cucumber sandwich, dabbed lightly with mayonnaise and surrounded by eight red grapes. Unsweetened ice tea, wedged with a lemon, sat on a coaster. No potato chips, pickles, or sodas. Daisy carefully removed the cucumbers and ate the mayonnaised bread. The butler entered the room, startled to find her already there. "Is there anything more I can get you?" he asked.

A big juicy hamburger, for one, she thought.

"No, thank you," she replied. She would simply have to remember to scout the pantry later for chocolate chip cookies.

After lunch, Daisy began to explore the gardens, careful not to step into any new flower beds. There were the rose beds, the perennials, the annuals, the shade and the sun flowers. Below the fountain, the water ran off into a small pond, dotted with water lilies sporting purple blooms. She found herself in awe of Mrs. DuMaurier's sense of taste, despairing that she could keep the place up to snuff in her absence. Then she remembered the gardener. He'd be the one to take care of all that. So pleasant was the afternoon sun and the slight nip of fall in the air, that Daisy quite forgot to keep track of time. She sat for the longest time on a stone bench near the fountain.

She heard the children arrive, before she saw them. Anthony came galloping out into the garden area, waving a picture. "Look, look, Mommy. I drew it for you." He thrust it into her hands and peered into her face for a reaction. A handsome looking boy with fine curly hair and long eyelashes.

"Why it's a picture of a—" Daisy studied the brown and red water-color blobs.

"A dinosaur," he said.

"Yes, a Tyrannosaurus—"

"Rex," he proclaimed.

"That's enough, Anthony. I'm sure your mother would like us to leave her undisturbed." A tiny woman with a wasp waist and oversized glasses reached down to take his hand. The children's newest nanny, Miss Agnes Madison.

"No, let him be," said Daisy. "Only he's got the dinosaur's name all wrong." She shook her head with mock sternness. "It's not Tyrannosaurus Rex, but Tyrannosaurus Wreck."

"But Mr. DuMaurier taught him to say Rex," Agnes persisted.

Anthony studied Daisy's face for an answer.

"Well then, it must be, if Mr. DuMaurier said so." Daisy smiled back at the tight, little woman with the fierce expression.

A red ball bounced into the conversation, followed by two-year-old Charlotte who tottered after it. Anthony kicked it into the pond. Charlotte watched the ball skip over the surface, then settle out in the middle. "But I want it," she cried, her ringlets of black hair bouncing in protest.

"Of course you do," exclaimed Daisy.

"How can we retrieve the ball?" Agnes addressed Anthony. It was lesson time, Problem Solving 101.

"Charlotte lost her ba-all. Charlotte lost her ba-all," sang Anthony, off-key.

Charlotte's mouth upturned, her eyebrows collapsed in the center, and her lips began to quiver. Thirty more seconds and she would be awash in tears. "I wan' my ball," she whimpered.

"Charlotte lost her ba-all," her brother chorused one more time for good effect.

Agnes yanked his hand. He had better be quiet if he knew what was good for him. The situation was definitely getting out of control, when much to the nanny's surprise, Mrs. DuMaurier stood up and announced, "I'll get your ball, Charlotte."

Kicking off her shoes, Daisy strode into the pond, all the way up to her thighs. Grabbing the ball, she threw it toward Charlotte. It bounced and disappeared down the garden walk, the two-year-old child waddling after it in hot pursuit. Slowly, Daisy sloshed out of the pond, the bottom of her dress dripping wet. Sopping footprints tracked all the way into the house, with a delighted Anthony and a disapproving Agnes following close behind. Agnes soon disappeared in her search for Charlotte.

As soon as Anthony had settled into the play room, Daisy slopped on into the bedroom for a hot shower and a change of clothes.

Dresses didn't much suit her anyway. She was happier in a pair of pants. Luckily, Mrs. DuMaurier had left a large closet filled with all kinds of different wear. It didn't take Daisy long to find a pair of light grey slacks and a soft, satiny, cream-colored blouse.

Agnes checked in to see if Mrs. DuMaurier wanted the children to eat dinner with them or should she feed them in the nursery?

"What time is dinner?" A little piece of information which the real Mrs. DuMaurier had forgotten to convey.

"Why, 6:30 as usual." Agnes stood in the doorway, patiently awaiting her orders.

"That's not too late for the children. I'd like them to eat with us. Then you can give them their baths." Daisy thought it safer to have the children around as a distraction. It would give her time to get a fix on Mr. DuMaurier. The thought of meeting him aroused both apprehension and curiosity. She had no faith in Mrs. DuMaurier's assertions that he wouldn't notice the switch.

Agnes didn't budge from the doorway. "But what about the hour after dinner when Mr. DuMaurier plays with the children? I really think it best that I give them their baths now."

I don't really give a damn when you give the children their baths, thought Daisy. "That would be fine. Do what you think is best."

The nanny queered her with a look. Perhaps the real Mrs. DuMaurier wouldn't be so lax with the staff, but it sure made Daisy uncomfortable having to tell Miss Agnes Madison which foot to put in front of the other.

It wasn't long before Daisy heard the front door shudder open and two male voices converse, the butler and, most likely, Paul DuMaurier. "Honey, I'm home," he loudly proclaimed from the bottom of the stairway.

Daisy checked her outfit one more time in the mirror. She had to admit that Catherine had done a good job. Even she would be hard pressed to point out the physical differences between them, except for one main facial feature: the smile. When Catherine DuMaurier smiled, there was something forced, tight in her expression, as if the human condition always contained a measure of necessary suffering. But when Daisy smiled, it was natural, full of glee and giggles, as if there was something inexpressively funny or absurd about life. To the mirrored reflection, Daisy said, "Remember. Be serious. Be profound. Gawd Almighty, I don't know if I can do this."

She found Paul in the study, his long legs stretched out before him, a newspaper held high in front of his face, a glass of scotch and soda by the leather chair. Daisy sucked in her breath and made her entrance. "How was your day?"

Paul scrunched down the paper. "Darling, you look beautiful. So good of you to ask me. Usually, you couldn't care less." A wry smile on his face.

Daisy stood there, stunned. From deep in the dark depths of movie theaters, she had worshiped the well-toned bodies and handsome faces of leading men. Seated before her was a man, the equal in looks of any one of them. Tall, wavy black hair, definitive eyebrows, dark eyes with long lashes, a lady-killer of a smile, flirtatious and kind, broad shoulders and a large chest, strong muscular arms and legs; the man was proportioned like a Greek god. It nearly took Daisy's breath away and certainly robbed her of her tongue.

"You look like you've seen a ghost, Cat." Paul twitted her.

Daisy expelled her breath. "No, you're as real as can be."

"I was the last time I checked. My day was hectic as usual. And yours?" He got up off his chair and pulled out a chair for her.

She felt hot, faint and dizzy all at the same time. It was good to sit down. *Gawd Almighty, I hope I don't drool.* She began to laugh at the image.

"Well, you seem to find something funny. I'm glad to see that you're feeling better." He sat back down on his chair. "In fact, you look a whole lot better. Can I get you a drink?"

I daren't, she thought, while shaking her head. *I just might make a bigger fool of myself.* She sat back, crossed her legs leisurely in the style which Catherine showed her, but which felt awkward, unbalanced.

Edward, the butler mercifully intervened and announced that dinner was being served. Agnes led the children into the formal dining room. They crowded around their father for big bear hugs before seating themselves on opposite sides of the table. The butler lit the candles and began to bring in supper: a leg of lamb, roast potatoes, peas, gravy, and mint jelly. He asked Mr. DuMaurier if he would like him to open a bottle of wine from the wine cellar, but Paul shook his head. While the children chattered about their day at play school, Paul carved the lamb. After serving each individual, the butler stood back, melting into the shadows of the room, but ready at a moment's notice.

Daisy reached over to cut up Charlotte's food.

"I can cut my own," announced Anthony, choosing to eat large pieces of lamb with bulging cheeks. He mashed his potatoes with his fork, slopped a huge quantity of gravy on them, and devoured them at breakneck speed. He nudged the peas to the side.

"Eat your vegetables, Anthony," Daisy said.

"No," the boy said.

"Do as your mother says," Paul echoed.

"I won't." The child's defiant tone surprised her.

"But why?" she asked.

He didn't answer. Anthony picked up a handful of peas and threw them on the floor. "You can't make me, Mama." The cry was both angry and agonized, with a long history behind it.

"Anthony, leave the table immediately," shouted Paul, rising to his feet. "I will not tolerate this kind of behavior."

For a moment, Daisy was afraid that Paul might hit the boy. The boy's expression switched from defiance to fear, lips trembling.

The butler advanced to clean the floor.

She held up her hand and gestured Paul to sit down. "It's all right. Edward, leave the peas on the floor. Anthony, stay in your seat." Then with a temporary truce declared and a wide-eyed Charlotte watching the whole drama, Daisy raised her peas on a fork and tasted them, licking her lips. "Among the sweetest of vegetables, aren't they, Paul?"

It took Paul a moment to shift gears, to back down from a glower to a glare. A question mark wrinkled his brow.

She gave him a knowing wink, all the while ignoring the truculent Anthony.

Paul nodded and followed suit, rubbing his tummy with a satisfied "Ahh," as he swallowed some peas. Smiling at Charlotte, he spoke, "Now it's your turn, baby girl."

Under the glowing, undivided attention of both adults, Charlotte scooped up her peas with the spoon and popped them into her mouth, imitating her daddy's "Ahhh" and rubbing her tummy.

Anthony hunkered down in his chair. No way were they going to force him to eat the vile stuff. But to his astonishment, they paid no attention to him, going about their eating as if he weren't even there. Finally he could tolerate it no longer. Slowly he brought the hated vegetables to his lips, swallowing hard, as if about to gag on the stuff. Then he took a second bite and a third bite, discovering that peas weren't so bad after all. He looked up from his plate to see both parents watch him with approving looks.

After they had finished dessert and were about to leave the table, Daisy leaned over toward Anthony and said, "Now, go pick up every pea that is on the floor, because you were the one to make the mess. We have to clean up our own messes."

Not willing to risk losing any more of his parents' temporary good graces, Anthony slid off the chair and crawled around the dining room rug, picking up each pea, as Edward stood by holding a silver tray. Meanwhile Charlotte dragged her daddy off to the playroom to show him her drawings. Agnes Madison soon collected the children to brush their teeth.

Daisy took a cup of decaffeinated coffee into the library, once again to wander around the room, scanning the bookcases. From way upstairs, she overheard a strong cry, "No, no, no, no! I'm not going to bed." It was Charlotte. Following the cry, she could hear the more muted voices of Paul and Agnes conferring.

Up the staircase, she trotted to confront the crisis. Agnes was counseling Paul: "It's important for her to go to bed at a regular time and to know that she can't manipulate the situation, Mr. DuMaurier."

"Yes, but she's scared of the dark."

"All children are scared of the dark. It's no reason to let them stay up beyond their bedtime."

"If I stay with her until she falls—"

"She'll never learn to conquer her fears, now, will she?" Agnes interrupted.

Meanwhile, Charlotte escalated from tears to howls of protest. Daisy entered her bedroom. Having kicked off her blankets, Charlotte sat straight up in the bed. "I'm not gonna sleep, Mama." Her little eyelids trembled with big tears.

Daisy brushed by the two adults and went over to the bedside. "Are you scared of going to sleep?"

Charlotte nodded.

Daisy lightly touched Charlotte's curly hair. "Do you get bad dreams?"

"I scared, Mama. The animals in the zoo get loose and come here."

"But the house is strong, Charlotte. They can't get inside."

"But I scared. I can't find you."

Out of the mouth of babes comes the real truth. Daisy nodded. "If you'll lay down and put your head on the pillow, I'll tell you a story."

"But where's the book?"

"Oh no, I'm not going to read you a story. I'm going to tell you a story from my own imagination. Now you have to promise one thing." Daisy gave Charlotte a serious look. Even the two adults stopped talking.

Daisy continued, "While I'm telling you a story, I want you to promise me that you will keep your eyes wide open, so that you can hear everything I say. Okay?"

The little girl sank back onto the bed, her head on the pillow, her eyes alert. She was safe now, no longer threatened by the shadows of the night. Her mother was going to tell her a story to drive away all the scary thoughts of abandonment and wild animals.

"Once upon a time," Daisy began, while nodding to Agnes that she and Paul could leave the room. Paul stopped on the other side of the doorway.

"Once upon a time, there was a little girl who never wanted to do what was asked of her. 'I won't, I won't,' she'd tell everybody, because she wanted everyone to know that she could say 'no.' When told to eat her supper, the little girl would say, 'I won't, I won't,' but then later her poor tummy became very, very hungry. When told to take her bath, she'd yell, 'I won't, I won't,' but then later her skin began to itch. When told to go to school, she'd say—"

"I won't. I won't," Charlotte answered.

"And then she grew very lonely, because she didn't have any friends to play with. At bedtime, her mother told her to keep her eyes wide open and what do you think she said?"

"I won't, I won't," repeated Charlotte, although her voice was beginning to soften and fade.

"Her mother said to her, 'I want you to keep those eyes wide open, so that you won't fall asleep and dream. Wide, wide open. And slowly, the little girl's eyes shut, while she continued to say, 'I . . .'"

"Won't." Charlotte's eyelids closed. Her sweet sleep breath sifted through the air.

Daisy pulled the covers up to the child's shoulders and tiptoed out of her room, softly shutting the door behind her. Paul was standing out in the hallway.

"Where did you learn to tell stories like that?"

She shrugged her shoulders. Any answer might tip him off that she wasn't the person he thought she was. Little did he know all her life she had made up stories to keep herself from being lonely.

Paul placed a hand upon her shoulder. "I have a hard time falling asleep as well. Perhaps you could come into my bedroom tonight, tell me a bedtime story too." The twinkle in his eye neither hid the huskiness in his voice nor the hesitancy of his invitation.

"I've plumb run out of stories this evening. Maybe another time." Daisy scurried off toward her own bedroom, before he could think up another strategy, but not before observing his eyes shroud over with hurt and despair.

Like a cold shaft of wind darting at her back, his voice chased after her. "I'm tired of waiting for those other times."

She closed the bedroom door behind her and put her ear to the door. She could hear him cross the hallway to his bedroom, yank open the door, and slam it shut.

Close call, girl, she said to herself. Her knees were wobbly; her heart was pumping fast.

Over the next few days, Paul kept his word and proffered no more invitations to his bedroom. He remained cool and distant toward her, unwilling to risk even mild flirtation. With the children, he couldn't have been more attentive or loving. Despite the long hours at work, Paul always took time off in the evening to play with Anthony and Charlotte. Agnes tried to keep them from intruding too much into their parents' routine, but she discovered that these parents kept sabotaging her best efforts.

Sometimes, Daisy would catch Paul studying her, observing the way she handled the children, a quizzical look upon his face. At those times, she consciously tried to imitate Catherine DuMaurier. Paul resorted to calling her "Catherine" instead of the pet name "Cat." Not a good sign for the marriage, but at least it simplified Daisy's life some.

After a week of polite if somewhat frosty interactions with him, Daisy found herself getting bored with the long night stretching ahead of her, the children asleep, and Paul ready to retreat to his own room.

"Want to play poker?" She had already discovered the cards in the library.

He looked up from his book. "But you don't know how to play cards."

"Sure I do." She opened a drawer in the nearby table and brought out a pack. She sat down in front of him and shuffled the deck. "Five card draw, jokers wild. We'll bet pennies. That way neither one of us will end up poor."

. He frowned, then picked up his hand. Repeatedly as the hours wore on, he won the pot. Winning did wonders in restoring his good humor.

Night after night, Daisy brought out the cards, sharpening her skills, until she became his equal. She learned that she could fake him out by pretending to be pretending. It was a complex strategy.

"I want to thank you, Catherine," he said on the fourth night.

"What for?"

"For no longer smoking around me or the kids."

"Oh," Daisy replied. She hated the stale, sour taste of cigarettes. They'd always made her feel sick to the stomach. "I've quit."

Paul's eyebrows arched. "Just like that? You always told me it was an addiction, that you'd never stop." He eyed her with bemused curiosity.

"A straight flush," she exclaimed, gleefully slapping the cards down on the table and distracting him in the process.

His mood toward her began to soften. As Paul dealt the cards on the seventh consecutive night of poker, his hand kept brushing against hers. Daisy knew she could pull her own fingers out of his reach, but something perverse, something exciting kept her right in the game.

"Oh gross. That's not her husband. She's going to get herself into heap of trouble," said Phoenix.

"But that's human nature," Kate replied. "We always want what we can't have."

"I want Carmelita," groaned Billy.

Phoenix rolled her eyes, then announced, "My dad's bisexual."

That got Billy's attention. "What did you say?"

"My dad likes to make love to men as well as women."

He shook his head. "Now talk about gross."

Phoenix laughed. "It doesn't bother me at all, but that's why he never married my Mom."

"He's with Talia, isn't he?" Billy asked.

"Talia is a transgendered male." Phoenix answered. "You know, a man who believes he's a woman inside. Mom says that way Dad's got the best of both worlds."

Billy still didn't get it.

Phoenix sighed. "Mom says that sometimes people are born with the wrong set of equipment. That they may be male on the outside but are female on the inside or the other way around. Now, do you understand?"

Billy shook his head. "You're either a man or you're a woman, far as I can see. So, your Dad is a fag?"

"Homosexual," said Katie.

"Bisexual," said Phoenix. "And that's okay, but sometimes, you know, he forgets my birthday and things like that. Mom says he's not ready to be a father, but I don't agree. He just hasn't had the chance, you know? So, I'm going to prove her wrong. Besides, she's too strict. Too many rules. Curfews, you know. Get real, you know."

"Sometimes you assume that we know things when we don't," Kate commented.

"Huh?"

Kate continued, "I promised I wouldn't correct your grammar, but I can't help noticing that every time you speak, you keep interjecting 'you know' into your sentences. The truth is, Phoenix, that we adults know a lot less than you think."

"I sure agree with that." Billy nodded.

"If you want your audience to hear the power in your message, then you need to cut out the 'you know' and tell us what you want us to hear." Kate smiled.

"Okay," Phoenix answered, pleased with herself for not getting defensive.

"I do that too sometimes," said Billy. "Didn't do too well in school. Kids called me 'dumb.' But I think I have one of them . . ." He couldn't find the right words.

"Learning disabilities," Kate interjected.

"Yeah. I think I got one of them." It pleased him to be understood. "I can't get my words right. I can't think things through. Like I don't know where I'm going right now, only that I'm getting away. I've always been pretty good at running away."

"It is true, Billy, that one needs to set goals and have self-discipline if one is going to get ahead in life."

"I always wanted to be a mechanic. Carmelita says it's dirty work. I've done construction work, but then you get laid off in the winter, and it's kinda hard on the body. When I first met her, I had big muscles from all the outside work." He flexed his right biceps for them to see. "But then I got this roll of beer flab. She doesn't like that none."

"Is she still doing it with other guys?" Phoenix asked.

"That's none of your business. No. At least ways, I don't think so." Blinking hard, he pulled the car over to the breakdown lane. "I gotta go and take a whiz." He jumped out and headed for the nearest tree.

"He's a mess." Phoenix said.

"He needs our help." Kate spoke in a soft, compassionate voice.

When Billy climbed back into the driver's seat, Phoenix announced, "Well, as long as you don't have any plans, why don't we drive west to the Pacific Ocean, maybe all the way to Seattle? That way, I don't have to take the bus."

"I've never seen the Pacific." He cranked up Matilda and turned onto the highway. "Sounds like as good a plan as any. Until I can think of something better."

He expelled a huge, sad sigh, full of despair and hopelessness. With worried faces, Kate and Phoenix exchanged knowing looks. It wasn't difficult to see that while Billy's brain might be heading westward, his heart was sinking south into the quicksand of dark human emotions. Even as Matilda crossed the border from Sarnia into Port Huron, Michigan, Billy understood that he was going nowhere fast.

SIX

MICHIGAN

Crossing the border between Canada and the United States, Matilda eased west onto the interstate, then veered north around Flint. Day had banked into evening, and it was time to find a motel near Bay City. They were all exhausted after a long day of traveling. Even Matilda seemed to welcome the layover.

"I can't afford to get us separate rooms," Billy announced, "unless you want to contribute some dough."

"Hey, we're the hostages, remember?" exclaimed Phoenix.

"I'm running out of money." He shrugged his shoulders.

"Phoenix and I can sleep in one room, you in the other. I will pay for the motel, but you pay for dinner." Kate didn't think it right to let Billy abdicate all responsibility. Phoenix was correct. This trip had not been one of their own choosing.

"But . . ." Billy began.

"We won't run away," said Phoenix, pleased that she wouldn't have to share a bedroom with Billy again.

"No, that's not it."

"You don't like to sleep alone?" Kate reached out and touched his arm. She knew the feeling well.

He shook his head. "It's just that, well, I was kinda hoping that one of you might read more of the book to me after supper."

Phoenix was about to protest that she wanted to watch television. But she, too, was curious about what was going to happen between Paul DuMaurier and Daisy.

"I'll read this time," said Kate. "That way we can give Phoenix's fine voice a rest."

Two bedrooms, supper in the belly, shower and bath, then a knock on the door. Billy entered for the nighttime reading. Phoenix snuggled down in her bed, with her head toward Kate, who was seated in the motel chair. With Kate's permission, Billy flopped down on her bed, grabbed a pillow, and curled up to listen to the less dramatic but more precise articulation of Kate Aregood.

"Now where are we?" she began, turning the pages.

Third Month

Once Daisy got the hang of it, she could see that she had a lot of free time on her hands. During the mornings and early afternoons, the children were off at their play groups, and afterwards Agnes Madison efficiently took over their supervision. Serena, hovering ever so discreetly in the background, seemed to know how the whole household worked. In fact, Daisy had to admit that she was beginning to feel a bit bored, useless. Never in her life had she been in such a position of ease. Frankly, it didn't suit her.

Spotting Catherine's computer in the upstairs study, Daisy became curious. In the local paper, the community college advertised computer courses and writing for adult students. The morning classes especially fit her schedule, so she signed up for four mornings a week. She figured that the writing class would force her to use the computer and develop her skills. Indeed, Paul was so busy with his work, that he never inquired as to what she did with her free time.

The real Mrs. DuMaurier had hired Agnes to be on duty whenever the children were present, even on weekends. Daisy wondered why any woman would be willing to work seven days a week, but the more she grew to know Agnes, the more she understood that the small, stiff woman didn't have much of a life outside of her duties.

Over a poker hand one evening, Daisy announced to Paul, "I've told Miss Madison that she's only to work every other weekend."

"Why, darling? I thought you could use the help with the children."

"It's not good for our babies to be spending all their time with her. Besides, I want us to have more time as a family." Daisy laid her cards down with a flourish: A full house.

Paul dropped his cards. "You beat me fair and square."

"I've set up a trip to the beach this weekend with the children. You're invited to join us." Daisy looked up at him, a twinkle in her eye, trying her very best not to be flirtatious but failing miserably.

"I've got a lot of work to do, but I could use some time off."

And so began a series of weekend outings for the DuMaurier family. First to the beach where Daisy dipped her feet into the chilly waters of the Atlantic Ocean, watching primeval horseshoe crabs scuttle on the sand. She taught the children about the sweet and succulent blue crabs of Chesapeake Bay in the South, how in a twenty-four hour period every year they shed their shells and hide, naked and vulnerable, from other predators until their new skin hardens into a bigger shell.

The children looked but couldn't find any such crabs on their northern beach. The family stopped at a lobster shack. Crabs she knew, but lobsters were another matter. Daisy had never eaten one before. To hide her ignorance, she delayed, watching how Paul dissected his meal, leg by leg, claw by claw, finally treating himself to the tail meat, dipping each piece into melted butter. The kids laughed to see the butter dripping down his chin. Before long all them were a mess to behold.

"I want to take them fishing," she announced one evening.

"But you don't know anything about fishing."

Of course, there was no way Paul could have known that Daisy, having spent so much time in the tidal waters, was a great fisherman. She feigned ignorance. "I can always learn. You can teach me." She'd leave it up to him to assemble the poles and equipment. Much to his surprise, she dug up the worms the very next day and deposited them in a big can of dirt for the weekend adventure.

"We could have simply bought the bait."

"Why, that would be a waste of good money, wouldn't it?" she said, drawing her last cards in the poker hand.

"I've never known you to be concerned with that fact. What's come over you, Catherine?"

Daisy took that opportunity as the moment to lay down her cards: A royal flush. "Gotcha," she exclaimed.

They took the children to Lake Baboosic in Amherst, New Hampshire. Fall was beginning to settle its colors around the quiet lake. The water was still warm enough for a quick swim.

"Watch out for the blood-suckers," Paul warned.

Of course, Charlotte refused to get into the water after that, but Anthony splattered about in the shallow section. He even picked off one leech from his skin, examining it with a curious eye.

"Ugh," said Daisy. "They're so ugly."

Paul pried another one off the boy's arm and threw it up on the bank. "A tasty morsel for the birds."

After egg salad sandwiches, cookies, and lemonade, Charlotte began to whine from fatigue. Daisy took her into her arms and began to sing the Alphabet song. She enlisted Anthony's voice and finally Paul's, until everyone was singing the silly verses. The kids slept in the car on the way back home, Anthony resting his head against one side of her, Charlotte on the other side. Daisy stroked the little boy's fine hair. Paul sat alone in the front seat driving, catching quick glimpses of his family in the back seat, a smile upon his face.

That night, they were too tuckered out to play poker. At opposite ends of the couch, they sat in the study, a soft fire burning in the fireplace. Paul sipped a brandy, while Daisy nurtured a cup of decaffeinated coffee.

"It was a wonderful day, Cat. The kids had a great time. So did I." He threw her a meaningful look, full of longing. The flickering flames cast a warm glow upon his face. His hand extended out to the middle cushion between them, an invitation.

She drank her coffee slowly. At first she thought it was heartburn, starting down in her chest, an empty, fluttery feeling, the kind which she sometimes experienced right before getting her monthly cycle. Sort of like dropping off a cliff. Oh, she knew what kind of cliff it was, the inexcusable, the most stupid thing a woman could do in her situation. Daisy had fallen in love with her employer's husband.

"I'm going to bed." She rose to her feet.

"Yes?" His question lingered between them.

It was what they both wanted.

No, Daisy reminded herself, *what Paul wants is to make love to his wife, and I'm not Catherine.*

"Good night," She turned to leave.

He reached out and grabbed her hand, got to his feet, and stood there, wanting to kiss her and holding back. She had not given him any encouragement. He dropped her hand.

"Good night, Cat." His voice was husky, kind, and sad.

She retreated to her bedroom but couldn't sleep. The moonlight filtered through the window, scattering light in all directions, stirring her restlessness. In bed, she tried to visualize her former boyfriends but, perversely, kept imagining Paul striding to the bedroom door, reaching out to turn the handle. She held her breath, hoping to hear his footsteps, but he did not come.

Daisy climbed out of bed, retrieved a pad of paper and pen, and seated herself by the window, looking up toward the moon. In the writing class, after studying the elements of plot, character, style, narrative description, her professor had asked the students to tackle their first assignment: the short story. The content could be anything the student desired.

What better time than this, when sleep is denied? Daisy set herself to the task. To her surprise, the words flew out of her imagination, flinging themselves onto the paper as fast as her pen would write. So absorbed was she in the process of writing that three hours fled by almost unnoticed, until she reached the last line of her story, "The Lunacy of Love." Daisy sat back and shook her aching hand after the feverish burst of creativity. Later, she would put it on the computer.

She read through the story one last time, a fierce tale of a young female toddler, discovered and raised by a pack of wolves. As the girl grew older, there was no suitable mate, so she left the wolf pack in restless searching for what she did not yet know. Roaming alone in the mountains, she finally spied a hunter. Told by her wolf parents to beware others of her own kind, she kept her distance, until she could no longer resist her curiosity. She crept closer to his campsite. The young man heard her tracking him, thought her a dangerous animal, and sent an arrow in her direction, piercing her heart. Only when he approached did he realize that he had slain a beautiful, young woman.

Daisy was surprised to feel the tears slip down her cheek as she finished reading the part where the young hunter held the dead woman in his arms and howled his own form of grief.

"What's the matter with me?" She peered out at the fading night sky, the drooping moon growing paler by the moment. It was not like her to be so uncertain, moody.

Little did Daisy know that Paul was asking the same question.

Over breakfast, he smiled at her. "I need your help."

"Sure. What do you want me to do?"

"I'm trying out some new personality test prototypes. I'd like you to be my guinea pig. They're do-it-yourself pen and pencil tests. I put you in a room, and you simply answer the questions as they apply to you."

"Today?"

"If that's all right with you," he replied.

After her morning class, Daisy drove to Paul's office. His secretary steered her to an empty room with a desk on which she placed several tests, pencils, and a cup of coffee. For over two hours, Daisy labored away, answering questions that were of the deepest personal nature and others that seemed totally irrelevant. At first, she thought she ought to answer the questions in the way that she imagined Catherine DuMaurier might, but quickly she could see how confusing that was. *Sometimes the best way to lie is to be mostly honest,* she reminded herself.

When she had finished that section, Paul arrived with sandwiches, chips, and a soda so that she could have something to eat during a thirty minute break.

The second part of the testing required his presence. "This is a marital questionnaire. I'll be asking you tough questions. Answer them as honestly as you know how."

"Okay." *Now, I'm going to have to really fake it,* she thought.

"One: how would you rate your marital satisfaction on a scale of one to ten, with one being not satisfied at all and ten being completely satisfied?"

This was going to be difficult. Daisy stalled for time. "Could you repeat the question?" *What would Catherine DuMaurier say?*

"On a scale of one to ten, how would you rate your marital satisfaction?" He sat there, showing no expression, pencil in hand to record her answer.

"I'd . . . give it a seven."

Paul didn't react at all, beyond inscribing the number on his sheet of paper. "And how would you rate your sexual satisfaction in the marriage?"

That was easy. "Zero."

Paul coughed, adding, "There is no zero on the scale."

"Oh, I mean one then."

"And, on a scale of one to ten, how would you rate yourself as a lover with one being a complete failure and ten being an expert?"

Daisy could feel her cheeks redden. She had never ever taken any psychological tests before, but she had agreed to be his subject. This was his line of work. "I don't know."

He waited.

"Give me a four." It's not like she'd had that much experience.

Paul carefully wrote down her answer. "On a scale of one to ten, how would you rate your husband as a lover?" He sat there, expressionless, looking at the paper.

"A ten, I'm sure," she blurted out.

A small smile appeared at the edges of his mouth, quickly replaced by a more professional demeanor. "How close is your marriage to being what you want it to be on a scale of one to ten, with one being a huge gap and ten being almost everything you would like it to be?" Paul stumbled over this last sentence, as if it wasn't well rehearsed.

"Zero," she answered.

That night, after the children had been tucked into bed and told their bedtime stories, Paul and Daisy regrouped down in the library. "Poker?" she asked but could see that he had little enthusiasm for the game.

He shook his head and sat down on the couch, patting the middle cushion. "Come over here, Cat. I need to talk to you."

There was no fire in the fireplace to distract his attention. Daisy sat down on the far end of the couch, facing him, her knees drawn up to her chin. He sipped at his brandy, gathering his thoughts as she waited for what he had to say.

"What's happened to you, Cat? You're so different. Some of those tests I gave you were repeat tests, ones that you've taken before. Nothing comes out the same. It's as if I am testing a different person."

I knew it. I should have tried to answer like Catherine. How was I to know she had taken those tests before? Daisy thought it wiser to remain silent.

"I watch you with the children, Cat. You used to be so impatient with them, irritable. Now they can't get enough of you. You play, sing, get right down on their level."

"That's okay, isn't it?" Maybe he believed that wasn't good for them.

"Hell, yes. Don't you remember how we use to argue about the best way to raise the kids? You told me not to coddle them or they'd grow up to be cry babies who'd insist on living with us into their dotage."

He looked sharply at her, as if trying to read her face, penetrate her eyes. She had on the blue tinted contacts. "And there is something else different between us."

Daisy's heart skipped a beat.

"This past summer I was thinking of asking you for a divorce. There just didn't seem to be any point to the marriage. But I couldn't see my way to taking the kids away from their mother. Nor could I ever tolerate living apart from them. Everything special between us had died, Cat. You weren't interested in me or my life. Nor did I have much understanding of yours. We lived in two different, separate worlds, you and I. That difference was exciting in the beginning, but there was no place for us to come together. And then, you suddenly changed."

Daisy waited, holding her breath. Perhaps she should tell him, make a clean break of it all. But she had promised Catherine DuMaurier.

A promise is a promise.

"You know you want to make love to me," he said. "And I want you so badly, Cat, that I can't sleep at night. I find myself pacing my room, wanting to tear down your door, and enter. It would be far more civilized if I simply knocked, wouldn't it?" He laughed at the image of himself, a wild beast on the rampage.

Yes, yes, yes, her heart answered, but her mouth clammed shut.

"I hold back. If I tap at the door and you don't let me in . . . Sometimes it's just better to turn away, rather than impale myself on pointed rejections. But I can read it in your eyes, Cat, something new. So, tell me," he said, "have you taken yourself a lover?"

Kate put down the book.

Phoenix expelled a large breath of air. "Why can't he see that she *can't* make love to him? I mean, it's not her husband."

Billy was quiet, disturbed by the story. He nodded toward Phoenix. "Do you think she ought to be listening to all this?"

"Oh, come off it. What do you think I am? A preteen? I know all about making love. It's no big deal." Phoenix turned to Kate. "Did you ever cheat on your husband?"

"Hey, you don't ask an elder that kind of question." Billy frowned.

"Oh, that's all right," answered Kate. "Yes, dear, I was married for a very long time to Horace Aregood. He wrote the gardening column for *The Washington Post.*"

"Gardening?" Phoenix found it hard to imagine that anyone would really enjoy digging in the dirt.

"Horace loved his flowers and bumble bees. He was a quiet man who enjoyed his routines and avoided conflict and change at all costs." Kate sighed.

Billy imagined it was a sigh of lost love.

Phoenix thought it elderly indigestion.

Kate knew it to be boredom.

"As for cheating, no, I was never unfaithful to Horace. At least in action." She arched her eyebrows.

"You mean you thought about other men?" Phoenix's eyes widened.

"Every married woman has romantic fantasies about men and other creatures."

Now it was Billy's turn to feel shocked, "You're funning the girl, ain'tcha?" It seemed downright indecent that a woman would be thinking about other men and "other creatures."

But Phoenix wanted to know more. "Were you ever asked by another man?"

Kate smiled. "Of course."

Phoenix pushed. "Who?"

"Ah, that's for me to know and only me. A lady never reveals that kind of information," Kate answered, "even if all the gentlemen involved are now dead and gone."

When Phoenix could see that no more was going to be said on the topic, she turned over in her bed, plumped the pillow, and closed her eyes. Kate rose from the chair, deposited *Double Trouble* on the bed stand, and straightened out Phoenix's rumpled bed sheets. Billy reluctantly rolled off Kate's bed and headed for his room. It had been a long day of driving and he was tired. He was grateful that the company of women and the book had kept his mind off Carmelita, but he dreaded the long and lonely night.

The next morning they headed up the eastern coast of Michigan towards Alpena. Staying on the interstate had made Billy nervous. He never knew when the police might realize that he had not only robbed a bank but kidnaped two women as well.

Alpena was a grey and depressing town, situated on Lake Huron. The people there seemed to move sluggishly, as if weighed down by the anticipated departure of warm summer days.

Reading the atlas, Phoenix stabbed her finger on the page. "Can we go see the Presque Isle lighthouse? Please, please, pretty please?"

Neither Kate nor Billy could stand her obsequious, squeaky voice. They agreed to the detour.

Two lighthouses perched in close proximity. A widow woman who had once lived in one of the lighthouses with her husband maintained a small museum of their years together alongside one of the tall structures. Outside stood a pair of stocks into which Phoenix insisted that Billy be confined while she took a photograph.

"What a great picture. The bank robber, the car thief, the kidnapper."

"Hush," whispered Kate. "Someone might hear you." She set Billy free.

"The stairs." Phoenix pointed to the entrance into the light-house. "Last one up is a rotten egg." She took off running, with Billy in close pursuit. They got to the top and looked out over the cloud-covered waters of Lake Huron. Billy could feel a deep gloom settle upon him, much like the fog that was rolling in off the Lake. "I'd have liked to have been a light-house keeper. To be left alone, not have to deal with the mess of women and things."

Phoenix rolled her eyes. Just when she was beginning to have fun, he had to go and start getting depressed.

Kate waited for them at the bottom of the lighthouse.

Afterwards, Billy slid into the driver's seat without saying a word.

Phoenix wagged her head at Kate to indicate that Billy had suddenly turned all moody. "Maybe we ought to turn west, huh?"

Without saying anything, Billy started up Matilda and headed westward toward Petoskey on the other side of Michigan. Although the fog seemed to clear, the more inland they drove, the blacker grew his mood.

"Why did she want me in the first place? What did I have to offer her? I've messed up every thing I've ever done. Carmelita was right smart to make me leave. I ain't never going to amount to much."

"Billy, there's a lot that's good about you," Kate said.

But Billy wasn't listening. He was on a roll downhill, determined to reach bottom where the mud and slime of self-degradation awaited him. The more "buts" that Kate offered, the faster he tumbled.

She began to fear for his sanity.

"Ah, come off it, Billy," complained Phoenix. "Get a life."

Whenever she got to self-pitying, her mother would always take the pragmatic approach and tell her to stop indulging herself.

Even that didn't work.

Billy simply inhaled Phoenix's words as rightful scorn, confirming him as a man who never could, never would get a life for himself. Lower and lower his mood descended. He bit his lips and tried to keep his thoughts to himself, but it was no use. It was like the two females could see right through him.

"Carmelita hates me. The cops hate me. Tell me what to do." Kate and Phoenix couldn't make a bigger mess of his life than he had already.

"Develop plans, set goals," answered Kate.

"Go west to Seattle," said Phoenix.

"I don't know what to do," he moaned. "Life isn't worth living without Carmelita."

"If you mention her name one more time . . ." Phoenix warned.

But Billy continued, "I don't know where to go."

"Seattle. To my father's place. That's where we're going."

"What good will that do?" he asked.

Kate recognized the sense of hopelessness, helplessness languishing behind his every word. Even the change of scenery from the fir forests and hay fields of mid-Michigan to the sandy coastline of western Michigan did nothing to elevate his dark emotions.

"Turn south," said Phoenix, atlas in hand. She was perfectly willing to take over the job as travel guide, now that Billy had abdicated all responsibility for his life.

Matilda dutifully swung south along the coast, through the prosperous towns of Petoskey and Charlevoix, past the large cherry farms and apple orchards, always following the coastline. Even Kate found herself distracted by the lush, changeable beauty of the landscape.

Billy brooded, inconsolable and silent.

"Would you like me to read some more of the novel?" Kate offered.

"If you want." He had no right to insist that the others be burdened by the darkness curdling within him.

Fourth Month

Paul continued to tease Daisy in a flirtatious way, waiting for a welcoming response from his wife. Daisy knew she ought to stop the poker games but reasoned that at least she was providing him with some form of companionship. She enjoyed spending the time with him. Each night, he edged closer to her, touching her hair, her cheeks, even rubbing her feet by the fire one time. "This little piggy went to market. This little piggy stayed home. . . ." He tweaked each toe in turn.

She squirmed as lava-like heat flowed from her toes to her thighs. It was as if his hands were electric, so charged were they with masculine energy. Daisy found herself swallowing hard, wondering if she could maintain the power to resist his charms. *He's not a free man. He's not my husband.*

"You know you want me, Cat," he said.

The name "Cat" froze the advancing warmth. "Cat" hissed at her and bit her hard. Each and every time, she sought a gracious excuse to back out of their physical contact.

Each and every time, Paul inched closer and closer, enjoying the game of courtship, taking all the time that was needed. He knew better than to hurry.

"I want us to put the marriage back together. I want us back in the same bedroom, Cat." His words pulled, then pushed at her.

"Give me time," she pleaded. *Give me another six months and then you can have your beloved Cat back in your arms.*

But Daisy knew that six months was too long a time, that something had to happen, that something was going to happen. Catherine needed to come home, but Daisy had no way to contact her.

In a panic, she threw herself into her studies, writing story after story of rebuffed and disappointed love. It wasn't the loss of control on Paul's part that frightened her. It was her own yearning, the temptation to give in, to kiss him, to give herself to him in a way she had never done with any man. The agony of yes and no, no and yes grabbed at her, like riptides that precede an immense tidal wave, pulling her down and threatening to drown her.

One night, Paul got up from the poker table, angled back around her chair, and began tracing a line up her cheek with his finger, teasing, tempting her. He curled a ringlet of her hair around his finger and smoothed his hand down the soft passage of her neck.

Daisy held her breath. She could feel her breasts lift in anticipation. Her throat constricted. She closed her eyes, both to deny the moment and to keep it forever.

"Cat." His voice was husky, appealing.

She grasped his hand, to prevent it wandering farther. *Cat. Why not Daisy? Why can't he love me?* She tried to peel his hand off her collarbone.

Instead, he bent his head and began nibbling at the back of her neck, his hand playing with her hand, intertwining the fingers. She could feel his lips upon her skin, sending up goose bumps of delight.

"No," she cried out.

"Yes, it's time," he answered, planting his mouth firmly on hers and pulling her up from the chair.

At first, and Daisy cursed herself afterwards for this, she yielded into him, returning his kiss and banking her body into his.

"Cat, Cat," he mumbled in gratitude.

She pushed him away then. "No," she said sharply. "It's not right."

"What do you mean?"

She struggled to say something intelligible, but nothing came. Daisy held up her hands.

"Goddamn it, you're my wife. What do you mean when you say 'it's not right.' You're playing games with me, Cat."

Cat, Cat, Cat. The name scratched across her psyche.

"It can't go on like this," she cried, fleeing the room.

That night Paul stayed down in the library, drinking whiskey by the glassful.

Daisy stopped the dangerous, nightly poker games. "I've got to study," she explained. She withdrew into herself, except around Anthony and Charlotte, converting all her hunger for Paul into maternal love.

Paul worked longer and longer hours at the office but was still careful to spend time each night with the children. Circles appeared under his eyes. He was drinking more, sleeping less. Love rebuffed curdled into anger.

One long and lonely night, after the children had gone to bed, Paul finished off his third whiskey. He intercepted Daisy as she descended the stairs for her nightly cup of decaffeinated coffee.

His words burst out, slurred and sour. "Talk to me, Catherine, damn it. Stop running away from me." He grabbed her arm.

"You're drunk."

"You bet I am. I'm tired of this charade. I want a divorce. I want to find a woman who can love me."

"Shush. The children can hear you," she whispered.

But it was too late. Upon hearing him shout, Anthony and Charlotte had crawled out of their beds and positioned themselves up at the top of the stairs, out of sight but in good listening range.

"I'm sick of this. I'm going to file for divorce in the morning." Paul kept his grip upon Daisy, knowing she would flee if she could.

"No, you can't do that."

"What good is a woman who won't go to bed with her husband? Why should I have to put up with that, when there are others who would be glad to be with me?" His voice rose in volume.

"If that's the only way we can stay married, then . . ." The thought drove her crazy.

"See, you don't even care whether I take a lover, do you? How could I ever have thought you loved me, Catherine? You don't even care. Well, goddamn it, I'm going to divorce you. As for custody, I'll take the kids as well."

"No-o-o!" Screams wailed from upstairs. The children began to howl and weep. "No, no, no. Don't Daddy. Don't!" They came tumbling down the stairs in an awful heap, awash in tears and panicky faces. Anthony grabbed onto his father's arm. "No, Daddy, no!"

Charlotte swept into Daisy's arms, scared, weeping profusely.

"See what you've done." Daisy glared at Paul. The children were hurt, and there was no excuse for it. She carried the weeping Charlotte back up to bed, saying, "It's going to be all right, honey. Mommy and Daddy will talk and settle all this. We love you and would never do anything to hurt you. It's going to be okay." A bold-face lie but it worked to soothe the little girl.

Paul took his son into his arms, his precious little boy. "I'm sorry." Guilt edged his face. What right did he have to hurt the children with his own selfish desires?

"Please, Daddy," Anthony begged. "Can't you and Mommy stay together?"

"Mommy and I haven't been getting along with each other. Maybe we need to spend time apart from each other."

"No, Daddy." Anthony dissolved into a little boy's tears. In between sobs, he hiccuped. "I love you both."

Paul carried his son up the stairs. "We'll have to wait and see what happens." He tucked the boy into bed. "Remember, we love you."

But these were adult words and did not reassure the child. The boy could only see his world was about to crack apart, and that the two people he most loved, most counted on, were about to leave each other. He did not think he could live if that were to happen.

Downstairs, the two adults sat apart on chairs, exhausted by the night's dark words and the weeping children. Neither one could look the other straight into the face.

"The children . . ." Daisy began.

"I'm so sorry." Paul sighed. It weighed on him, the effect of his words etched on their panicky young faces. Never before had he hurt his children with such devastation.

"A divorce . . ." Daisy tried to spit out the words.

Paul shook his head and cut her words short. "Not now, Catherine. I can see that. Maybe someday. I won't pursue a divorce right now. Nor will I continue to bother you with my demands."

Daisy felt relief that a divorce was no longer imminent. She could not tolerate her having lost the marriage before Catherine returned to patch it up. But his last words, words of defeat, scared her. She remembered what he had said about the other women in his office.

Like a storm that has come and gone, the debris of their relationship floated about and clogged their feeble attempts at conversation. It was late when they each headed off to their separate bedrooms.

Daisy stopped to check on the children. Charlotte was sound asleep on a pillow, still damp with her tears. She entered Anthony's bedroom, adjusting her eyes to the room's darkness. Snuggled down into his bed was his large teddy bear, all alone, its button eyes vacantly staring at the ceiling.

Anthony had vanished.

Kate slapped shut the book's covers. "End of the chapter."

Matilda merged into the traffic of Traverse City, a city situated at the fork between two peninsular legs: Old Mission and the Leelanau Peninsula. For no apparent reason, Matilda took a turn northwest toward Suttons Bay in the Leelanau Peninsula. It was as if Billy, having given over all direction in his life to others, was now even ready to let the car drive itself.

"Anthony's sorta like me, running away," said Phoenix, "although a four-year-old boy can't take care of himself."

"Think how scared Daisy and Paul DuMaurier must be. Perhaps as scared as your mother has been these past three days?" Kate arched her eyebrows.

"Yeah, but she'll get over it." Phoenix didn't want to think about her mother.

"I wonder if *she* ever thinks of me?" Billy interrupted. He didn't have to explain who "she" was.

"Of course, she does," Kate reassured him. "Why don't you call her?" Kate spotted a red telephone booth in Suttons Bay. Perhaps that would jerk Billy out of his depressive state.

Billy guided Matilda to a curb spot. He sat there, drumming his fingers upon the wheel.

"Well?" Kate tried again.

"Do you think she'd really want to hear from me?"

"I'm sure of it. Now go on, call her. Phoenix and I will stretch our legs and give you some privacy."

"But I'd like to listen," Phoenix said.

"Sometimes a man has got to do some things for himself. Come along, Phoenix. Maybe later you could call your mother."

"No way." She scrambled out of the car.

As they turned to look back, they could see Billy heading slowly toward the red telephone booth, searching his pockets for change.

Down one sidewalk on the main street and then up on the other side, they walked. While Phoenix browsed Enerdyne, the science store full of mechanical gadgets and mental games, Kate took special interest in the marina and the small office buildings below the main street. After thirty minutes, she retrieved Phoenix and returned to Matilda.

Billy was nowhere to be found.

"Where could he be?" Phoenix shaded her eyes against the bright afternoon sun and looked up and down the street. They started walking around the town.

Down by the public beach, they found him standing like a statue. Something was wrong.

"What happened?" Phoenix asked. "What did she say?"

Billy didn't answer.

Kate placed her hand on his arm. "Are you all right?"

Numbly, he shook his head and wiped his cheeks with the back of his hand. He didn't want to talk and open himself up to more hurt.

"The call didn't go well, did it?" Kate stated the obvious.

He nodded and continued staring out at the water.

"Did she get angry at you?" Kate could only guess at what had happened.

He shook his head.

"Was she sad?"

He swung his head side to side in mute despair.

Kate was confused. What had caused such grief?

"Did you talk to her, Billy?" Maybe he'd been unable to reach her.

"She wasn't there."

"Did someone else answer the phone?'

His face and neck muscles tightened.

"A man?" Kate asked.

He nodded.

"That two-timing bitch," Phoenix said.

Billy shrugged his shoulders. "It's what I deserve," he muttered, moving toward the water. He pulled away from their comforting touch. "Take the car. It's yours anyway. What's left of the money is in the trunk."

"What are we going to do?" Phoenix glanced wildly at Kate.

Billy shucked off his shoes and socks, then stepped into the Lake, hesitating briefly as the chilly water lapped at his pant legs, then his thighs, then his waist. He kept moving forward, teeth clenched.

"Do you know how to swim?" Phoenix yelled.

He didn't answer. No one had ever cared enough to teach him to swim. But that was okay. *Drowning's like falling into sleep. It'll stop the pain.*

"I'm going after him." Phoenix was frantic.

Kate placed a restraining hand upon her arm. "Sometimes, a person has to force himself to the edge of things." *Better that he come to terms with his feelings than let those emotions drive him to a mental station from which he could never return.* "Besides," she added, "the water is quite cold."

With waves slapping against his chest, Billy kept moving forward to the promises of eternal sleep. The water flowed onto his shoulders, his neck, and then over his mouth. He stood on this toes to keep his nose free, but soon ran out of ground. One more step and he would be over his head. Only then did Billy feel the arctic fingers of cold digging in his flesh, clutching at his heart. A moment of utter clarity flashed into his consciousness:

I'm not ready to die.

He heard his Mama's voice shouting angrily in his brain. "What in the hell are you doing, son, out in the middle of a freezing lake? Have you lost your cotton pickin' mind?" His teeth chattering violently, his body shaking uncontrollably, his legs like pillars of cement, Billy thrashed back to the safety of the beach.

Phoenix ran up to him. Head bowed and dripping wet, he peered miserably at Kate.

"Before you die of pneumonia, let's get you a towel, another pair of pants, and some hot tea." She sent Phoenix to the car for Billy's clothes and guided him to the public restrooms. With Phoenix standing outside while Billy changed clothes, Kate hurried to the red telephone booth to make two strategic telephone calls. She returned before he even knew of her absence.

They all walked to a nearby coffee shop where Kate ordered tea for herself, cocoa for Phoenix, a double mocha cafe latte for Billy, and three large raspberry scones.

Kate checked her watch. "Eat up quick. We have an appointment to keep."

The two of them looked at her.

"I've made an emergency appointment with a Dr. Meggie O'Connor, a clinical psychologist in town. I told her that someone in our group was very, very depressed."

"But I can't talk to nobody like that." Billy sucked up the last of his latte.

"Of course, you can. Phoenix and I'll come to the session with you. I said we're all family. Fewer questions that way. I mean it wouldn't do to say we had been kidnaped by you, now would it?"

Phoenix grinned.

"But what about the police?" Billy had never been able to talk feelings.

"Well, I don't think it's a good idea for the psychologist to know our real names, so I've given us all pseudonyms. I hope you don't mind, Billy, but I told Dr. O'Connor that your name was Paul DuMaurier." Kate sat back, taken with her own cleverness.

"Paul DuMaurier?" Billy frowned.

"I want to be Daisy," Phoenix exclaimed, clapping her hands. "I can be his kid sister."

"All right," said Kate. "I guess that leaves me with the name of Catherine DuMaurier, Billy's mother."

"You can't be Mama," said Billy. "You're not at all like her."

"Phoenix, you'll have to be his daughter," Kate continued. "because you're much too young to be my child."

"Well, don't think you can treat me like I'm your kid afterwards," Phoenix warned Billy.

"I don't get it," he said.

"We're all playing parts from the novel, but changing the relationships," Phoenix explained. "Kate is Catherine DuMaurier, who is your mother, and I'm Daisy, your daughter."

"I don't get it," repeated Billy as they dragged him off to the psychologist's office.

"It's simple. Your name is Paul DuMaurier, and you're depressed. You have a wife, named Carmelita, who is driving us all crazy," Phoenix said.

"But I'm Billy Pickle."

"No, you're Paul DuMaurier," the two women answered.

"And I'm married to Catherine?" He frowned.

Phoenix rolled her eyes. "No, you're married to Carmelita and she's driving you cuckoo, buggy, crazy, out of your head."

"That's for sure."

Kate paused at the door to the therapist's office. "Say nothing to Dr. O'Connor about the bank robbery, our real names, or how we know each other. I'm your mother, Catherine. Phoenix is your daughter, Daisy. Otherwise, tell her everything else." Kate opened the door.

"Dr. O'Connor?" Kate extended her hand to the psychologist.

A woman in her early forties smiled at them but focused in on Billy. "You must be Paul DuMaurier? Your mother telephoned and said that you needed to be seen immediately."

Billy nodded.

"Please, come into my office." After they all sat down, the psychologist asked, "Now, how may I help you?"

They sat in a semi-circle facing Dr. O'Connor. Kate spoke first. "I'm Catherine DuMaurier and this is my granddaughter, Daisy."

Billy looked puzzled.

Kate looked at him with great concern. "We're dreadfully worried about him. Paul finds it difficult to talk but he's been having a terrible time. Especially marital difficulties."

"With Carmelita," added Phoenix.

Billy lowered his eyes to the floor.

Kate continued, "In fact, today, we were afraid that he was going to end his life. That's why I called you."

"Is Carmelita your wife, Paul?" Dr. O'Connor asked.

Billy pursed his lips.

"Son," Kate spoke sharply. "Dr. O'Connor was asking you about your wife."

"She doesn't love me anymore," he answered, head down.

"When he telephoned her this afternoon, a man answered," Kate interjected.

"I see," said Dr. O'Connor.

"She kicked him out. Told him that he had to bring more money home and—" Phoenix said.

"That's enough, dear," Kate interrupted. "The less said, the better."

"All right, Granny," Phoenix replied.

Kate cut her eyes at her.

"Let me understand. The three of you are on a vacation trip?" Dr. O'Connor knew that they weren't from Suttons Bay. Something odd about the way they communicated to each other. Probably just another dysfunctional family.

"In a manner of speaking." Kate smiled.

"We're taking me to Seattle to see my . . . my other parent," Phoenix answered.

"Oh, so Carmelita isn't your mother then?" Dr. O'Connor was beginning to sort it out or, at least, she thought she was.

"Hell no! That bitch."

"Phoenix, Daisy, I mean. Watch your language," Kate said. "My granddaughter here has never gotten along with Carmelita, and we thought, Paul and I, that it would be better to send her to her mother in Seattle. I've been telling her she will be like the phoenix that rises out of the ashes, when she's no longer around her stepmother." *An excellent recovery for my slip of tongue.*

Billy raised his head, as if he couldn't quite believe what he was hearing. "Her mother?"

Kate sensed that things were about to spiral out of control. "Let's not get sidetracked. The pressing problem is not between my granddaughter and her stepmother, but between my son and his wife."

"Whom you don't really like either," observed Dr. O'Connor.

Her insight caught Kate by surprise. "Well, that's true. I'm not the kind of mother or mother-in-law who interferes, but Carmelita has treated him in a very shabby fashion. I must beg your forgiveness, son, but I think she's truly a trashy sort of a person." There. It was out, and Billy was simply going to have to hear it.

"I gather the three of you are planning to continue your travels to Seattle then, after this session?" Dr. O'Connor was trying to understand the limits of what could be accomplished.

They each nodded.

"In that case, I think I would like to meet alone with Paul and listen to what he has to say about the situation. If more needs to be done, I will let you know." Dr. O'Connor stood up and opened the door.

Kate gathered her pocketbook and exited before Phoenix. As the teenager passed by Dr. O'Connor, she couldn't resist whispering, "Daddy is a dork, if you know what I mean."

In the waiting room, Phoenix sidled near the therapy door to eavesdrop, but Kate pulled her away. "It's between them now. Let's go find an ice cream sundae. I've had just about enough excitement for one day."

"All right, Granny."

"You can drop that affectation right now," Kate said.

"I don't know. I kind of like being Daisy."

Back in the office, Billy squirmed under the singular focus of Dr. O'Connor. But the woman had a kind and soft voice that promised understanding.

"Tell me about this Carmelita."

"She's beautiful. A face like an angel. And I think it was a mistake, maybe a joke from the Big Man Upstairs that she wanted to be with me. At least, in the beginning."

"So, there was a time when she loved you."

He nodded. "But I lost my job, and her favorite thing was to shop with her girlfriends and buy things an' we didn't have no money. I was looking for work but . . ."

"Does she also have a job?"

"No. She told me from the beginning that she's an old-fashioned lady. That she loved the way I took care of her." Billy chose his words carefully, trying to sound halfway intelligent.

"And when the money wasn't forthcoming, she threw you out?"

"Kinda. I mean, I had the key to the apartment, 'caz I still did all the laundry and the grocery shopping. That ways I could keep an eye on her. I got a few odd jobs, but nothing like a salary, like before."

"Let me understand, Paul. You were the sole breadwinner for the family, yet when you lost your job and had to resort to day work, you still did the grocery shopping and the laundry?"

Billy nodded.

"And she continued to shop with her girlfriends?"

Again, he nodded.

"Is she disabled, sick, or otherwise unable to work?"

"No." These questions weren't going the way he thought they would.

"Is that a habit of yours to let people take advantage of you?" Dr. O'Connor's voice turned sharper.

Billy squirmed in his chair. He had expected sympathy, not this. "But I love her." He knew his response sounded both dumb and true.

"You didn't answer the question, Paul. Loving someone doesn't entail letting them stomp all over you. You've been separated how long?"

"Twenty-five days, four hours, and thirty-six minutes." He counted on his fingers.

"And already, there's another man in the apartment." Dr. O'Connor was acting like a coon dog, having treed its prey.

His shoulders slumped with defeat. "That's why it's better that I—"

"Kill yourself?" Dr. O'Connor was going to start baying for sure, any minute now.

He flinched but nodded.

"Then she'd be really sorry, wouldn't she? She'd cry over your grave, weep, and feel badly about how she had mistreated you."

Billy couldn't believe that Dr. O'Connor could see right through him. Yes, he had worked out that grave scene, envisioning Carmelita all decked in black.

Dr. O'Connor continued, "She might even don widow clothes."

"But she'd be really sorry," he answered.

"Yes, maybe for a day or so, Paul. But what you refuse to understand about yourself is how very angry you are at her. Your fantasy of killing yourself is your way of exacting revenge upon her."

"No," he said, his voice sounding weaker and weaker.

"And from what I understand of Carmelita, it's a wasted gesture, one that will have very little effect on her. If it's anger you want to express, then you must choose a way that will have an impact." Dr. O'Connor was staring straight at him, challenging him.

"But how?"

"Let me borrow an insight from the Native American culture. As a young man, you're given a secret, spiritual name.

The name isn't one that describes how you are as a person but rather what you can become. Over your life span, you learn to live into that name, into that vision of yourself. If that vision is a small one, then you'll always be trying to fit yourself into a name that constricts you, holds you down, imprisons you. But if name is large enough, well, then the whole world awaits what you have to offer."

He struggled to understand. "But my name is—"

"Paul DuMaurier," she said. "Yet perhaps, you have another, hidden name that tells more the truth of who you really are."

He nodded.

"With a strong name, there can be a direction in your life."

"Can I make it up?"

"Perhaps what you need to do, Paul, is to try on several names. See what fits you. Remember, no one but you has to know what that name is."

He nodded.

She drove home the point. "So, the choice is yours. Take a good look at what you want to do in this life, then create the vision for yourself, find your name. Or kill yourself now and never know the adventure."

"But what about Carmelita?" He knew he sounded like a broken record. *What about my love for her? What about my anger?*

"The best revenge," Dr. O'Connor replied, "is simply to get on with your life with a sense of dignity and purpose. That alone will tell her how badly she has treated you. That alone might make her realize what a good man she lost."

He had to agree it made sense to him. Hope began to nudge aside his feelings of shame. He, Billy Pickle, could make a new life for himself, one of which he could be proud. But then the memory of the bank robbery loomed up, dispelling his brief anticipation of something new, something different for himself. *I'm nothing but a common criminal.* The shame returned fourfold. He looked away from the psychologist.

"You're pulling yourself back down," she observed.

"But what if I have done terrible things?"

"And who of us hasn't done terrible things? It's part of the human condition, Paul. Find ways to make amends. By learning from what you did, you change your life so that you will never do those things again."

Billy gritted his teeth. "I can't even do the bad things right."

"Do you still feel like killing yourself?"

He shook his head.

Make amends. Live a life of honor. He'd try to find a way to pay the money back, somehow. That way, he could begin to feel good about himself. Maybe even to dream about a future. "And Carmelita?"

The therapist didn't answer.

Billy sighed. "I've got to say 'goodbye' to her, don't I?"

She nodded. "It's not easy, Paul, to say goodbye to someone you love. But when loving is so hurtful, then it becomes like a poison inside. I think you have a lot of love to give someone who can appreciate it, someone who will love you no matter how hard things get."

How can there be anybody else? Billy had his doubts.

Dr. O'Connor continued, "Now what you have to learn is how to love yourself enough to create a strong dream for your life."

"And a name to live into," Billy added. *If only I had a way with women like Paul DuMaurier.*

Dr. O'Connor looked at the clock, indicating that their session was over.

"I guess I owe you something for your time."

"One hundred dollars will cover it."

He blinked. He'd been expecting her to say twenty dollars or something like that.

"Unless you have insurance," she added.

He still carried insurance from his old job but couldn't tell the psychologist that his real name was Billy Pickle, that he was a wanted criminal. "I gotta go to the car and get the money. It'll take just a minute."

He returned with one of the few one hundred dollar bills that he had gotten in the robbery. He rationalized, *This is just a temporary loan. I'm gonna pay it all back.* He handed the new bill to the psychologist.

She smiled. "Suicide is an expensive proposition."

"I know whatcha mean."

She held out her hand. "Goodby, Paul. Good luck with the rest of your life. It's a fine thing to have a mother and daughter who obviously care so much about you."

Billy shook her hand. He'd have liked to have told her the truth, that his real name was Billy Tyler Pickle.

He found Kate and Phoenix browsing through a clothing store. Billy announced, "Okay, I'm ready to get moving again."

They piled into Matilda and headed southwest along the coast, past the towns of Lake Leelanau and Glen Arbor, arriving at the Sleeping Bear Dunes just as the sun was starting to edge over the horizon.

"Will you look at that mountain of sand?" exclaimed Phoenix. "Let's climb it."

Billy had to admit that he was feeling pretty good. Somehow, Dr. O'Connor had restored hope and strength to him, even as she had depleted his bankroll. "Okay," he said, swinging into the large parking lot. "I'll race you up to the top. Winner treats to dinner."

"Count me out," said Kate.

They persuaded her to call out "one, two, three" and charged up the large dune. At first, Phoenix drew ahead, each foot sinking deeply into the sand for purchase, her youthfulness lending her that initial burst of speed.

Billy knew that he couldn't afford to let the scrawny teenage girl beat him at a footrace. His heart pounding hard and lungs gasping for breath, he surged forward to the top. She arrived two seconds later.

"Your treat," he said.

"No fair," she answered. She knew she had lost. "Okay, but I get to choose where."

To her surprise, Billy reached over and gave her a big, affectionate hug.

"Hey," she yelled at him, knuckling him on his shoulder. "Come on." She grabbed his arm and yanked him down the dune, running so fast, she fell, rolling over and over in the sand.

He tumbled too, laughing all the way to the bottom.

"Jack and Jill," said Kate. "You're both covered with sand. You're not getting into Matilda until you shake it off."

They traveled to Ludington and bought ferry tickets over to Manitowoc, Wisconsin. Dinner at a hamburger joint was quick. They would sleep in the car while on the ferry.

"It's a hard way to travel," said Kate.

"But every minute, we're getting closer to Seattle," announced Phoenix.

Billy stepped out of the eatery to purchase a postcard of Michigan. He penned a quick note to his wife:

Dear Carmelita,

We're taking a fairy boat across the big lake. I'm with some freinds. Bye,

Billy

He looked at the postcard, then xxxxxed out his name and scrawled "*Paul*" instead.

SEVEN

WISCONSIN

It was a short night for the boat ride, a long night for the sleepless Kate. As the ferry boat churned its wake across Lake Michigan toward Wisconsin, she paced the deck, thinking that this was no way for an eighty-two-year-old woman to embark on an adventure. She couldn't help worrying that if and when the police finally caught up to Billy, there might be a fatal shoot-out in which one or all three of them could get killed.

Billy managed to get in about three hours of sleep, sitting straight up at the wheel of the car. Phoenix had moved from the back seat of the car to the front where she promptly fell asleep.

Kate's return to the car woke them up. "I can't sleep," Kate complained, sounding grumpier by the moment.

Billy yawned and stretched.

Phoenix sat up and stared ahead into the ferry's cargo area, still caught in a half-twilight stage of consciousness.

"It's a lot more comfortable up on the enclosed deck," Kate said. "There's coffee and sandwiches."

"Coffee?" Now that caught Billy's attention.

"Peanut butter and jelly sandwiches?" Phoenix came to life.

"My treat," said Kate. As an after-thought, she picked up *Double Trouble* for entertainment. "Let's find out what happened to Anthony. No use wasting valuable time counting sheep."

Neither Phoenix nor Billy had the heart to tell her that they hadn't been suffering from insomnia.

"Do read, Phoenix. You have such a good, strong voice," said Kate as they settled on deck chairs, sandwiches and coffee in hand.

Phoenix, tongue working furiously, excavated the peanut butter from the roof of her mouth.

Eighth Month

High and low, they searched the house for the little boy, but there was no sign of him. Paul even began to consider the possibility that Anthony had been kidnaped. His conscience tortured him. Softly, Daisy tiptoed through the neighboring yards and gardens, calling out "Anthony," until her voice grew hoarse and daylight edged over the horizon. No sign of the child.

"We'll have to call the police," Paul said, eyes furrowed by deep circles. He had looked everywhere.

"He's around here, somewhere." But Daisy had run out of ideas.

Together, the two of them returned to the house and kitchen to make the telephone call. There, amidst the smells of crackling bacon and eggs, stood Serena, serving up a hot plate of pancakes to the little boy, seated at the table.

"Anthony," Paul cried out, "where have you been? We've been searching all over for you."

"Hush now," barked Serena, "you've been making too much of a fuss already. Let the poor boy eat his breakfast."

Anthony eyed his father guardedly.

"Where—"

Paul didn't have a chance to finish, before Serena interrupted him. "After you both squabbled, this child was afeared for his very survival. The two people he most loves can't even find a way to be civil with each other. So he comes to be with me, 'caz he knows I'm gonna take care of him. An' I can't rightly blame him." She stood there, hands on her hips, much like an angry mama bear defending her cub.

Paul knew better than to offer explanations.

Daisy seized the moment. "I don't want a divorce, Paul."

Now Paul had two strong women looking right at him, demanding to know his intentions.

"Please, Daddy." Anthony began to sniffle.

"I'm sorry, honey." He knelt down by his son's chair. "I didn't mean to scare you. I won't divorce your mama. I promise."

Daisy breathed a large sigh of relief.

"Now you two sit down and eat your breakfast. I've got a mess of pancakes and eggs cooked up to perfection." Serena was taking charge. "Then we'll have to wake up Charlotte. I'm sure she'd like to hear the good news too."

Over the next few days, Paul apologized repeatedly to the children. He resumed a polite demeanor toward Daisy but kept a physical distance. He took the kids on adventures without inviting her. Sometimes, she would catch him looking at her, studying her when he didn't think she would notice. Most of the time, he acted as if indifferent to her presence.

She dove into her writing and computer courses, studying at night while he played with the children or drank alone in the library. Often, he would call and say he had to miss dinner as he was working late. Sometimes on the weekend, he would be gone for half a day, again working.

At Christmas, he gave her a thousand dollars. "Spend it on whatever your heart desires."

The present didn't even come close to what her heart desired.

Daisy kept her feelings in check, telling herself over and over that this was for the best. The comfort of sleep escaped her. She took an aerobics class, hoping to keep her body occupied with sensations other than the memory of his hands upon her skin. She ran four miles a day, developed lean muscles. She enrolled in an advanced writing class.

But she was miserable. *I just need someone to love. Someone of my own.*

In late November, she had bought a collie pup and named him "Scalawag." Anthony and Charlotte became great pals with the puppy. Scalawag didn't seem to mind when Charlotte twisted an ear, pulled on his tail, or hugged all the wind out of him. He licked their faces, barked, and chased them around the yard, until they all ended in a tumbled heap. At Christmas, he ate the boxes that held their gifts and peed on the Oriental rugs. Everyone agreed that he was adorable.

He's the children's dog, she decided. Scalawag had made it his mission to keep herd on the youngsters. *But I need someone that's solely mine.*

After New Year's Day, Daisy adopted a female kitten with black fur and white paws. She dubbed her "Buttons" due to her clear brown eyes. Buttons immediately attached to Scalawag, stalking and batting the puppy's tail every time it wagged. The kitten didn't seem to hold it against the puppy when he'd step on her.

Charlotte immediately abandoned Scalawag to Anthony and claimed Buttons as her very own pet. "She mine," the little girl announced. Charlotte dressed Buttons in doll clothes, an activity barely tolerated by the kitten.

Daisy then bought two green parakeets. She called them "Bill" and "Hillary." Unfortunately, Hillary caught a cold in her second week at the DuMauriers. Daisy found her lying on her back in the cage one morning, her legs sticking straight up in rigor mortis, with Bill worriedly pecking seeds around her. The children held a graveside ceremony for Hillary, trying to think of appropriate things to say about her, as they buried her in an old shoe box.

"Nice tweet," said Anthony.

"Pwetty bird," added Charlotte.

"Goodby, Hillary," said Daisy.

Agnes didn't think much of all this fuss for a bird. When Bill collapsed and keeled over a week later, she flushed the bird down the toilet. "Death can be overly traumatic for children," she explained to Daisy.

Daisy bought four goldfish the next month but soon grew bored with their tedious swimming, round and round in circles. It reminded her too much of her own life.

Paul didn't pay much attention to the influx of new pets. He'd absent-mindedly pat Scalawag, complain about cat hairs on his favorite library chair, whistle at the birds, and totally ignore the fish. What Daisy found most disturbing, aside from his polite indifference toward her, was that Paul had begun experimenting with colognes and a new hair style.

She remembered what he had said about the other women in his office.

To make it even worse, Paul continued to keep up social appearances, expecting Daisy to accompany him to the winter cocktail parties of his associates. Daisy tried to pick out the most devastatingly beautiful outfits from Catherine's closet with jewelry to match. A bright red foot-length gown set off with ruby earrings for the Christmas season, a midnight-blue velvet dress with plunging neckline, sapphire necklace, and matching earrings for late winter, a short, satin emerald shift to highlight her trim legs, and an emerald ring surrounded by diamonds for springtime. She'd carefully apply Catherine's make-up and, studying her profile in the mirror, knew she was as beautiful as she could be. But nothing snagged his attention.

He continued to make polite conversation. "You look very attractive tonight, Catherine." That would be it.

It's for the best, she thought but had trouble convincing herself.

At the cocktail parties, women swarmed around Paul, drawn to his charisma and sense of humor. Nor did he discourage the extra attention. After making sure that his wife had someone with whom to converse, he'd make the rounds. Like a magnet, the women congregated in his direction, laughing at his self-deprecatory jokes, touching him on the arm in familiar gestures. Flirtatiousness exuded from him naturally, unconsciously. Paul had a way of convincing every woman that she was the sole and fascinating focus of his attention.

Out of the corner of her eye, while some other man would be boring her with statistical detail or political gossip, Daisy would watch Paul like a hawk, noting how much attention he was returning to the individual women. She knew she had no right to be jealous.

It's only a matter of time, she reminded herself, *before he'll find another woman to love.*

The thought drove her crazy.

How can I love him? How can I keep him faithful for Catherine?

It was like the old days in high school when she and her girlfriends would strive to remain "technical virgins." *Would it be possible to do that with Paul, to keep herself from making love to him, while loving him all the same?*

Daisy knew she had to do something. She rationalized that all her behavior was out of concern for Catherine's welfare, but her heart knew better.

On the way home from one such party, Daisy asked Paul to drive to the scenic overlook fronting the Atlantic ocean. The early spring night was cold enough that the parking area was deserted. The stars twinkled brightly. The surf was up, spraying salty white foam over each wave. Daisy slipped off her party shoes and climbed out of the car.

"Where are you going?" Paul asked.

"To the beach." With her heavy coat flapping in the brisk night wind, Daisy ran down the sandy embankment towards the water.

Keeping on his shoes, he followed her across the sea grass.

"Catherine, it's cold out and time to go home to bed. I'm tired."

She flung off her expensive coat and let it drop to the sand.

"Catherine," he said in a tone of annoyance.

She started laughing.

"You're going to freeze to death. By God, I didn't know you had drunk so much at the party. You must be sloshed." That was the only explanation that made sense to him. She was beginning to shiver in the cold. He took off his coat and positioned it over her shoulders.

As he straightened out his coat upon her, she reached up and planted a delicate kiss upon his lips, taking him by surprise. The taste of her mouth was sweet, inviting. Daisy's body slipped into the contours of his body. His hands gripped her, first inside the coat, then along the seam of her dress, until their knees folded simultaneously. They sank down onto the sand. He touched her face, caressed the length of her, his hands greedy for what had been so long denied.

She banked into his body, her body arching with its own primal fire, her lips hungry for his. His legs entwined with hers. She could feel his hands groping for her silken underwear, and she knew that the moment would soon pass when she could say no.

"Whoa," she said, pushing him back, catching her breath, and wanting to disrobe all at the same time.

"Now or never, Catherine," he said. "I can't keep doing this."

She hadn't meant it to go so far. Honest-to-God, it was a mistake. She pulled herself out from under him and managed to stand up, shaky, weak at the knees.

I love you, Paul.

You're not my husband.

I've gotta get out of here.

One, two, three, these thoughts assailed her. Without saying a word, because she could no longer trust herself, Daisy turned away, retreated up the beach, retrieved her sandy coat, and silently dusted it off. Silently, Paul passed her on the way to the car. She could tell, by the tight line of his shoulders, the grim set of his jaw, the avoidance of his look, that she had finally done it.

Not a single word on the way home. He slammed the car door shut and preceded her into the house. He slammed the library door. Only a stiff drink would calm his rage.

Daisy ran up the stairs to Catherine's bedroom and flung herself upon the bed. Sleep never came. The next morning, she stayed in bed to avoid seeing him over the breakfast table. She sent word down to Serena to bring up a breakfast tray.

Serena found her crying and fussing into a pillow.

"What's the matter, Sugar?" Serena put down the tray, sat herself down on the edge of the bed.

"Oh, if you only knew."

"But I do know," countered Serena. "You aren't Miss Catherine, if that's what you mean."

Daisy sat up, stared at Serena.

"You is somebody else."

"How did you—"

"I've known Miss Catherine all her life, her every little mood, her way of talking and acting. You weren't here but a couple of days, and I could see, in them little ways, how different you was from her. Now, Miss Catherine might think she can keep some secrets from this old woman. Hah! Never could. She was right unhappy, ready to bolt like a high-strung filly, and I figure she finally got to do what she wanted to do. And here you is, in her place. It amazes me that her husband don't notice the difference."

"But he does," Daisy exclaimed.

"Then you best tell me all about it."

Daisy spent the rest of the morning detailing the whole ruse to Serena from beginning to end, without explaining why she had been crying.

Serena, however, didn't miss a trick. "You're in love with him. What you going to do about that? He don't belong to you."

Tears began to form again in Daisy's eyes.

"He's Miss Catherine's husband," Serena continued. "Only she don't seem to want him much."

"I don't know what to do. Maybe I ought to pack up, go back to where I came from."

"But then the children won't have a mama, will they?"

Serena was right. It wouldn't be fair to Anthony and Charlotte for her to suddenly abandon them. "What am I going to do? There's still four months before Catherine returns." Daisy simply couldn't see how she could last that long. It was an impossible situation. "Serena, tell me what to do."

But it wasn't Serena who had an answer to that question.

It was a sudden, unexpected call from the real Catherine DuMaurier.

The engine of the ferry changed pitch and began to slow as they approached Manitowoc, Wisconsin.

"Well," said Kate, "what do you think is going to happen?"

"I've changed my mind," Phoenix announced. "Catherine's a creep; she's going to barge into the story and ruin everything. I think Daisy ought to go ahead, have sex, and get it over with. Besides, she's a better parent to those kids any day."

"But remember," Kate said, "Daisy made a promise and promises are important to her. Daisy has to stay in character."

"At least she's there for the children, which is more than you can say for some parents," Phoenix added.

"I feel sorry for Mr. DuMaurier," said Billy. "I know what it's like to be pushed away again and again by a woman. You know, you could only take that so long, before you kinda lose interest, if you know what I mean." He raised his eyebrows at Kate to indicate matters above and beyond an adolescent's comprehension.

"Like it's not something you can always control," he added. "So that even if you wanted to, you can't."

"You're referring to problems with the plumbing, I presume." Kate arched her eyebrows.

"An' things stop working for awhile, an' you worry it'll never happen again, you know?"

"But it all comes back eventually, doesn't it? When you're no longer so hurt or angry." Kate smiled.

Phoenix rolled her eyes. "Mom calls it 'impotence,' and the two of you don't have to talk about it as if I don't understand what you're saying. It's when you can't get it up."

Billy visibly shrank into his shoes.

"What else has your mother said to you?" Kate was intrigued.

"That some men even think there are teeth in the vagina."

"I never did," Billy exclaimed. Apparently there was still some men in the world who were more screwed up than he.

"She also said that diabetes can cause it to happen," Phoenix continued, "But you know what I think?"

"I'm very interested," Kate answered.

"I think it's like when a woman is angry at a man, she doesn't want to make love, and so when it's the other way around and he's angry at her, then his you-know-what says 'no way.'"

"How astute of you," said Kate.

"Can we change the topic of conversation back to the book?" Billy's face was growing redder by the moment. "I think Mr. DuMaurier ought to divorce his wife, because he loves Daisy, not Catherine."

"Yes," said Kate, "but Paul believes that Daisy *is* Catherine."

All three agreed it was a terrible dilemma.

Just then the boat's horn sounded. They had arrived at the docks. The three of them clambered down the metal steps to the cargo area, where Matilda patiently awaited them. After a long series of mechanical groans and moans, the ferry finally lurched to a stop, lowered the bay door to the dock ramp, and disgorged the cars.

It was still dark, pre-dawn, and the travelers were tired from a long night. After refueling, they headed west and south toward Lake Winnebago and the city of Fond du Lac. The morning sun began to dust the hilltops of the rolling countryside, dotted with white dairy barns of fieldstone foundations. Each scattered small town along the way sported a Catholic church on one corner facing a dance hall/tavern on another. Store window signs advertised the advent of various polka bands.

In the early morning light of the countryside, farmers were letting their cows out of the barn. Billy observed, "When I was a kid, I wanted to own a bunch of milkers. Mama used to say it's going to be a hot day if all the cows stand under a tree, but if it's going to rain, they'll all lay down."

"Cows are stupid," Phoenix said.

"When I was a child," Kate said, "I dreamt I was going to be a cowgirl. Since there weren't any horses for me to ride, I'd jump on top of dairy cows. I'd ride them back and forth across the pasture. The only problem was that the cows started producing butter instead of milk."

She waited for them to laugh.

They didn't.

"Maybe I ought to get a farm," Billy said.

"Maybe," Kate answered. "You've got to figure out what's important to you and do what you love."

"But not until you get me to Seattle first," Phoenix interjected.

Matilda skirted Lake Winnebago. A brisk breeze was kicking up some good-sized waves. At Fond du Lac, the three travelers stopped over for some breakfast and cleaned up in the restrooms. Billy ate an enormous breakfast: three strips of bacon, two fried eggs, a stack of pancakes, and three cups of coffee. Kate stuck to bran cereal with skim milk, while Phoenix ordered a melted cheese sandwich. Kate paid for the meal.

After leaving the restaurant, they headed westward, past small cheese factories, one-room red school houses, and long grey buildings. At the town of Waupun, Billy pulled the Dodge Dart over to the side of the road and pointed to the prison, a large fortress-like building with guard towers.

"I've been thinking," he said, "about what that psychologist in Michigan told me. About making amends for what I've gone and done. I've been thinking a lot about that, about the bank robbery and all. Maybe it would do me good to stop here, go up to that prison there, and give myself up. You know, take my punishment like a man. Then afterwards, I can be free to do what I want, like work on a farm."

"Are you crazy?" Phoenix couldn't believe how dumb Billy could get.

"You two take the car, go onto Seattle without me." He opened the driver's door. "I mean it ain't even my car."

"What about Carmelita?" Phoenix racked her brains for something to keep Billy from doing something incredibly stupid.

"She don't want me no more. I know that now." His voice was strong, almost heroic in resolve. Determination had replaced the depression. Billy stepped out of the car and started walking down the road.

"Kate," Phoenix said, "we've got to do something."

"I'm trying to think. He's determined to do the right thing. Only that's going to get him into a lot more trouble." She got out of the back seat, then climbed into the driver's seat. Kate inched the car forward in the breakdown lane, following Billy toward the prison gate.

"Please, Billy." Phoenix leaned out of the car window. "We need you."

Billy shook his head, shouting back. "This is something I've got to do. Mama always told me that it's better to tell the truth than keep living a lie." He kept on walking.

"Kate," Phoenix begged.

"Oh, how I hate to do this," the old woman replied. But nothing else came to her. Kate stabbed the accelerator with her foot, rocked the car wheel back and forth, and forced herself to hyperventilate. Matilda wove passed Billy, jerking forward and braking at one and the same time.

Billy ran after the wobbling car.

"Help, Billy!" Phoenix called out the window, signaling for him to catch up to the moving automobile.

"My chest, it hurts. Oh, it hurts," cried out Kate, in a voice loud enough for Billy to hear.

"Quick, turn off the motor," Billy yelled to Phoenix.

Kate's eyelids fluttered, as she let herself slump in the seat. The car shuddered to a stop.

Billy flung open the car door to examine a semi-conscious Kate.

"My heart . . ." Kate sputtered.

"Help me move her over," Billy ordered. Together, he and Phoenix pulled Kate to the passenger side. Billy jumped into the car.

"What are you going to do?" Phoenix was really worried.

"Take her to a hospital. There's got to be one somewhere around Madison." Billy gunned Matilda out of the break-down lane. "Hold on. I'll get you help before too long."

After ten minutes had passed, Kate coughed and sat up straight. "Oh, I feel so much better. A hospital is unnecessary. Probably just my hiatal hernia."

"You sure about that? You didn't look so good." Billy didn't really trust Kate's self diagnosis.

"I'm embarrassed. I've caused you two so much trouble." She coughed a few times. "Every once in a while, I suffer a bad case of indigestion, and it mimics a heart attack. But you know, one simply can't recover from a cardiac arrest so quickly."

"Phew," said Phoenix. "For awhile there, I thought Billy was heading to prison and you to the morgue. Then where would I be?"

Kate took a long, deep breath. *Time for confession.* "It isn't necessary for you to make amends, Billy, by giving yourself up to the police."

"I robbed a bank, didn't I? I took money that didn't belong to me."

"Yes, but restitution of that money has already been made."

"Huh?"

Kate coughed again to exhale the lingering effects of her hyperventilation. "I sent a check for the amount of the stolen money to a friend in Miami in an overnight mailer. I asked her to anonymously deliver that money to The National Trust Bank in Washington, D.C. with a note in Spanish, apologizing for the inconvenience caused by the robbery. So, you see, Billy, there's no need to turn yourself in to the police." Kate folded her hands.

Billy's mouth dropped open. He stared at her.

"Mind you, it's simply a loan. One that I expect you to pay back with interest."

For once, even Phoenix was at a loss for words.

"But how did you know how much it was?" Billy asked.

"I made a discreet telephone call to the bank, told them I was a reporter for the USA Today News, and asked them the amount that was taken. I think I covered all the bases."

"How long do I have to pay it all back?" Billy didn't really trust the news. Nobody had ever been that good to him.

"As long as you need. I figure that Horace's life insurance has gone to a good cause.

"I don't know what to say."

"Then it's better not to say anything. Let's have no more discussion of either prison or penitence."

"So I'm free and clear?"

"You don't owe the bank any money," said Kate.

"You're still a criminal," said Phoenix. "I mean, you can't just buy your way out of bank robbery and kidnaping."

"But nobody got hurt," added Kate.

"What happens now?" he asked.

"We're going to Seattle," Phoenix declared.

"It's as good a plan as any." Kate smiled. Billy needed some time to digest the change of circumstances.

"Are you sure your heart's okay?" he asked.

"It's never been better. There's nothing wrong with my mind either," Kate answered.

"I'll be damned. I don't know what to say." He shook his head.

"You might try 'Thank You,'" suggested Phoenix.

"But how do you thank someone for saving the rest of your life?"

"By living a full and genuine existence. That is what I expect from you," answered Kate. "Now enough of this. I don't handle compliments well."

Billy sat back, exhaling a big sigh of relief. He was off the hook with regard to the bank, though maybe not with the kidnaping. There would be time enough to worry about that later.

Swinging north of Portage, the ground began to change character, turning sandy. Potato farms with large irrigated fields replaced dairy farms. The Wisconsin Dells signs dotted the roadside. "Ride the Ducks!," "Mini-golf," "Robot World," and "Tommy Bartlett's Ski Show" billboards beckoned them toward the rock bluffs and scenic narrows above the Wisconsin River.

"Please, please, pretty please," Phoenix began.

"No," said Billy

"Amen," answered Kate.

Enough excitement for one day. They stopped only long enough for Phoenix to purchase a "Wisconsin Dells" tee shirt for each one of them, a not-so-subtle bribe.

It didn't work.

They traveled westward on roads paralleling the interstate. Frequently, large semi-rigs barreled up behind Matilda, having detoured off construction bypasses. Every time the trucks rode her bumper, Matilda choked down into an old lady's crawl. But as soon as the large rigs backed off, gave her decent space, Matilda would zip ahead like a perky new sports car. She zoomed through small towns filled with barbershops and cafes, advertising apple or lemon meringue pie.

Billy's stomach grumbled.

Past the town of New Lisbon, the landscape turned flat with scrubby woods and soil that didn't look good for farming. Off to the west as they moved closer to the Driftless area near Tomah, hills appeared. The nearer they drew to La Crosse, the steeper the hills. Matilda seemed to welcome the challenge.

Meanwhile, Phoenix sank into a terrific pout, arms crossed, exuding sourness with every breath. "I've always wanted to see the Wisconsin Dells," she muttered.

Kate exchanged glances with Billy. "Phoenix, you could be an actress. Would you do us a favor and read from the novel?" Kate didn't know whether she would be willing to take the bait. But if Phoenix would read, Kate could then enjoy the passing scenery.

Teasing Phoenix took Billy's mind off tart lemon pies. "I bet the real Mrs. DuMaurier is gonna throw a hissy fit when she finds out that Daisy's been after her husband."

"Daisy isn't *after* Catherine's husband. It's the other way around. It wasn't her fault she fell in love." Phoenix picked up the book. With dramatic entrance, the teenager read the last sentence where Kate had previously stopped.

It was a sudden, unexpected call from the real Catherine DuMaurier.

Daisy immediately recognized her voice. "Thank heavens you called."

"Are the children okay?"

"Yes, but—"

Catherine cut her off. "I'm coming home early. I'm sick and in need of medical treatment. It'll take me some time to complete the paperwork in this god-forsaken hole of a country."

The telephone crackled in Daisy's ear. It was difficult to hear Catherine, as her voice wavered in and out of audible range.

"So . . . coming home . . . soon as possible. Leave now . . . some pretext . . . address . . . reach you . . . very sick." The line went dead.

"Hello? Hello? Are you still there?"

There was no reply.

Daisy didn't even know from what country Catherine was calling. But the urgency and desperation in her voice were clear.

Rummaging in the attic, Daisy retrieved her shabby suitcase held together by rope and broken locks. There wasn't much to pack, except the clothes she had brought north with her. She took one look at her dull old duds and tossed them into the trash can. Then she pulled them out. "I best get used to them." It would be impossible to keep up the style of the real Mrs. DuMaurier. Way beyond her means.

Serena entered the bedroom.

Daisy blurted out her conversation with Catherine. "When should I leave? I'm not sure when she'll reappear. What am I going to tell the children?"

"That's not what's bothering you, and you know it." Serena busied herself, choosing some of Catherine's outfits and packing them in Daisy's bags. "It's only right that you take some of these clothes. Miss Catherine wasn't all that partial to them anyways."

Numb, Daisy slumped down upon the bed.

Serena continued, "It's not the telling of a story to the children that's eating on you. It's the saying goodbye to them. It's the saying goodbye to him as well. You ain't never going to see them again, and you knows it. That's what's hurting inside. And only time's going to heal that wound."

Daisy doubted that even time could be that strong.

"So you best be to doing it quick and getting on your way. The children are still eating their breakfast." Serena shut the suitcase.

Reluctantly, Daisy rose to her feet. Serena was right. If a copperhead bites you, you have to cut the flesh quick and suck out the poison, because if it swirls about in the blood overlong, you'll faint to the spot where you're standing.

"Charlotte, Anthony." She spoke their names upon entering the kitchen. "Your mother has to take a brief vacation."

"Why, Mommy?" Charlotte's voice whined with anxiety.

"Because . . . because Mommy has to do a photography assignment." It was the only plausible explanation.

"When will you be back, Mom?" Anthony asked.

Never, my brave Anthony. Never, my sweet Charlotte.

"Oh, I don't know. Probably two weeks," she lied.

That seemed to satisfy them. They returned to their bowls of cereal, with Agnes Madison there making sure they ate to the very last, soggy piece.

"Have you seen Mr. DuMaurier this morning?' she asked the nanny. *Might as well get over the tough part of saying goodby to him.* Inside, she felt her heart beginning to shred.

"He's already departed for work."

Breathing a silent prayer of thanks, Daisy knew she was a coward. She didn't know if she had the strength to say goodbye to him. Never again would she see his smile, watch him play with the children, feel his arms around her.

She wrote a note and placed it on his desk:

Dear Paul,

I was called out of town for a special photography assignment. I'll be back as soon as I can.

Daisy hesitated, chewing on the end of the pen. She added another line, knowing at least this time she could tell him the truth:

I love you, Paul. No matter what happens, I will always love you.

She couldn't bear to sign it "Catherine." Nor could she allow herself the indulgence of signing it "Daisy."

Instead, she wrote:

From your poker partner.

The children came running up to her. It was time to get their morning hug from her before going off to preschool. Daisy fought hard to keep tears from surfacing. She did not want to burden the children with her own grief. She embraced them and kissed them on their cheeks, saying, "I love you with all my heart." They tumbled out the front door, following Agnes.

"What are you going to do now?" Serena presented her with the suitcase and a bag of freshly baked cookies.

"I don't rightly know," said Daisy.

"You're not going back to that ole diner, are you?" After Daisy's previous confession, Serena knew everything about her.

"I don't know, but I can't stay here." Daisy needed to put as much distance as possible between herself and the DuMaurier family.

"Did you leave your forwarding address in Miss Catherine's dresser drawer? She's got to know where to send you that money."

She gave Serena a big hug. "Of course, she does. Two hundred thousand dollars is nothing to sneeze at." But Daisy had left no such contact information. She knew that unless she made a complete break of it, she might never be able to leave. *It's my own fault that I fell in love with him and the children. My own damn fault.* The only way to set it right was to leave forever. Two hundred thousand dollars wasn't going to buy back her happiness.

She shook food into the goldfish bowl, patted Scalawag and Buttons goodby, grabbed a carnation from a kitchen vase, picked up her suitcase and the bag of cookies, exited the large house, and dropped the flower onto the parakeets' graves. Serena stood at the window, waving until Daisy walked out of sight.

Nothing was left of her in the DuMaurier house.

Not even an address.

"That's about the dumbest thing I've ever heard." Phoenix slammed the book shut. "No way would I ever disappear without collecting the money."

"Sure ain't chickenfeed," added Billy.

"But what's more important to happiness, love or money?" asked Kate.

"Money," said Phoenix. "If you have lots of it, people will love you to death."

"Money," answered Billy. "When you're starving, who cares about love?"

"You two don't believe in romance?" Kate frowned, then noticed that they were both grinning.

"We're just funning you, Kate," he said. They both started laughing at her.

"Oh my, I took the bait, didn't I?"

Matilda zipped into the river town of La Crosse.

"We'll be crossing the Mississippi river soon," Kate said.

Phoenix peered out the window. "I don't see it. I don't see it. Oh," she noted. "There it is." The car crossed a bridge over a small body of water.

"I thought the Mississippi was supposed to be a big river," Billy protested.

"That's a channel. There, now you can see the Mississippi." Kate pointed ahead to the large river full of boat traffic.

"Holy Moly!" Phoenix cried out.

Spanning the mighty Mississippi, a series of thin metal bridges stretched up and down the river, precariously stapling Wisconsin to the state of Minnesota.

EIGHT

MINNESOTA

"I'm starved, and if you guys don't stop the car soon and let me eat lunch, I'll turn into a freaking werewolf." Phoenix turned toward Billy.

"You okay?" Billy looked at Kate, concern etched onto his face.

Kate nodded. Hunger pains were also gnawing at her insides, causing a bad case of indigestion. *It's what I deserve,* she thought. *The lies we tell often become the truth we live.*

"I get to choose where we eat. I spoke first," said Phoenix.

"Whadda'll it be?" Billy asked.

"A cheeseburger deluxe." Phoenix immediately spotted a fast food carry-out. "We don't even have to stop to eat. We can park, pee, pay, and push off."

His eyebrows arched in puzzlement.

"I'm being alliterate." Phoenix stuck her nose in the air.

"Illiterate?" Billy asked.

"No, that's what *you* are." She glimpsed Kate's frown in her peripheral vision. "You know, using words that all begin with the same letter."

Kate nodded. "You're correct in your application of language. However, there are some observations that are best not made. Now, I suggest that since we are going to eat at Phoenix's restaurant of choice, we have a sit-down meal. It's the civilized way of dining." It had been a long time since she had allowed herself the sinful treat of salty french fries.

Both Billy and Phoenix couldn't believe their eyes when Kate ordered one diet coke, one unadorned hamburger, and two large orders of french fries which she proceeded to drown in ketchup. Billy scarfed down two fish sandwiches and one medium fries while slurping a large chocolate low-fat shake, much to the disgust of Phoenix. She pushed back her chair, disassociating herself from the odd couple and concentrating on extricating the plastic toy in the kid's meal she had ordered.

"Awesome. A dinosaur. Wouldn't that kid, Anthony DuMaurier, like this?" Phoenix feigned an attack on Billy with the toy.

Billy belched. "'Scuse me."

"Gross," Phoenix said.

Kate dabbed the last of her fries in the pool of ketchup. "What do you two think about Daisy's departure without any way for Catherine to send the money?"

"Ways I see it," said Billy, his mouth full of sandwich, "she done earned that money fair and square. It's hers. Maybe she'll let Catherine know where she is when she gets where she's going."

"What I don't understand," Phoenix interjected, "is why she didn't leave an address."

"I have an idea about that." Kate paused for dramatic effect, waiting for them to prompt her to tell more.

They didn't.

Billy peered into the bottom of his shake to see if his straw had sucked it dry.

Phoenix surveyed other teenagers in the restaurant.

"Guilt." Kate plunged ahead. "Daisy felt guilty for having fallen in love with Catherine's husband."

Phoenix shook her head. "It was pride. She wanted to show them that she didn't need the money. She could make it on her own. Be her own person, live under her own rules."

"I wonder," Billy asked, "if Carmelita will declare me dead, now that I'm gone."

Phoenix rolled her eyes. "Time to move on."

Kate dabbed her mouth with the napkin, slowly stood up, and waited for her legs to adjust before moving. The french fries weighed as heavily upon her conscience as on her stomach. "If you'll drive, Billy, I'll do the reading."

They gassed up Matilda and headed north, paralleling the Mississippi River. Phoenix inclined her head on the back of the seat, closing her eyes as she listened to the precise, reassuring voice of Kate Aregood.

Tenth Month

Catherine DuMaurier returned home in terrible shape. She was having to pay dearly for her months of liberation from family responsibility. The deep tan from the African sun did little to camouflage the yellowish tint of her skin. "I must have picked up a bug on this last shoot," she explained to Paul. It took all her energy to pretend that she was just temporarily under the weather and had only been absent a short time. She kept to the arrangements of separate bedrooms and donned loose clothing to hide the dramatic loss of weight. Her face, abdomen, and ankles, however, bloated with edema.

The children were more than delighted to see her. "Mommy, Mommy, Mommy." They whooped in glee, falling all over her like a pair of young puppies. After bestowing a big hug upon each child, she gently disengaged them. It hurt to be touched.

The house she had left was not the same one to which she returned. Where did this god-awful menagerie of animals come from? Didn't Paul remember she was allergic to cat hair, that dogs track mud throughout a house, and that goldfish are dreadfully boring. Thank heavens, there weren't any birds. Perhaps Agnes or the gardener could eventually be persuaded to take the dog, the cat, and the fish. And where did that girl leave her forwarding address? That was the biggest puzzle of all. She couldn't very well ask Paul, could she?

Paul, at least, was the same. Polite, distant, and a devoted parent. Catherine laughed. *And to think how Daisy was so worried about Paul foisting his affections upon her.* Between severe bouts of nausea, Catherine searched the house high and low for Daisy's address. *Perhaps she means to call me in a few days.*

"You don't look well, Catherine. Is something the matter with you?" Paul knew it wasn't normal for a flu-like "bug" to last this long.

Catherine could hardly bear to join them at dinnertime. The sight of food made her want to retch. "So you've noticed?" A flicker of a smile crossed her face.

"Have you seen a doctor?"

"We have to talk, later." She nodded knowingly over the heads of the children.

Once Anthony and Charlotte trotted off to bed under the prompting of Agnes Madison, Catherine entered the study. She sat on a chair, facing Paul. "Life never works out the way you expect, does it?"

"What do you mean?"

"I saw a specialist at the Mass General Hospital this morning. He said that I had picked up a rare foreign infection which is now eating away at my kidneys. There doesn't seem to be any antibiotic available to stop the process."

"I don't understand. I thought you had the flu."

"The prognosis isn't good." She threw back her head in regal fashion.

"Come on, be serious."

"I am serious. I'm going to die."

A crazy thought assailed him: *It's as if Catherine has prepared all her life for this dramatic moment.* "You must be mistaken. What about a transplant?"

"The physician put me on the list, but I'm not counting on it. Number one, I've got a rare blood type. Number two, people aren't falling over dead in order to donate their kidneys to me. Where could they ever find a suitable match?"

"What about dialysis? We could get another opinion."

"I've already thought of that. The MGH specialist is the fourth physician to confirm the disease. Dialysis will work for a short period only."

Paul ran both hands through his hair. How was he going to tell the children? How would he take care of them when she was gone?

As if she knew what he was thinking, she said, "I'll tell Anthony and Charlotte in the morning. Believe me, I don't want to die, but sometimes you simply have to face the facts."

The next day, Catherine gathered the children and with Miss Agnes Madison in attendance, she explained. "Sometimes a person gets sick and they don't get better. And when that happens—"

"They plop over," Anthony chirped, "like Hillary."

"Like Hillary." Catherine bided her time, not having the slightest idea in the world who in the hell was Hillary.

"An' then Bill too." Charlotte's large eyes brimmed with sadness. "He wen' away."

Agnes Madison cast a meaningful glance toward Catherine and, behind the children's backs, she pantomimed the flushing of a toilet.

Catherine knitted her brow. She was now thoroughly confused by the children's rambling and Miss Madison's peculiar gestures. She began again, "Well, sometimes a person gets so sick that she or he goes away forever and ever."

"But they come back?" Anthony squirmed at his mother's feet.

She put her arms around him. "When a person dies, that person never comes back. And that makes the people who love that person feel very very sad."

"Mommy, are you sick?" He stared straight into her eyes, his fingers on her cheek,

Catherine whispered softly, "My brave, brave little boy." It was all she could say and still maintain control. Agnes swept the children out of the room.

To Serena, Catherine later confided, "I guess it is simply a matter of waiting. I'm so very tired these days. I'm not worried about Paul. He'll soon find himself another wife, but the children. Oh God, the children. I must stay alive as long as possible for them."

Catherine began the exhausting dialysis treatments. Paul bent over backwards to give her fresh flowers every day, favorite foods to entice her to eat. He sat at the side of her bed for hours, talking with her, remembering their courtship. "When I first saw you at the gallery, I thought you were the most beautiful creature on this earth. You were mysterious and divine, the star in the New York world of photography. I was so happy when you finally agreed to be my wife."

Catherine recalled why she had first fallen in love with him, the boyish grace about him, the looks of adoration that melted her natural reserve. What had happened to that wonderful time of romance when they were all fire and passion? When had indifference slithered into the relationship? Was it the children and their time demands? Did the loss of libido creep on the heels of familiarity? Was it the giving up of her own career to become a mother and wife? Or was it Paul's success at each and every venture, pulling him more and more away from her? Now, at night she could hear him retreat down to the study to drink. And then she recalled why she had stopped loving him. It was when he no longer had made the effort to break through her self-imposed barriers.

She was amazed at how much Charlotte had grown during her absence. The negativism of the earlier stage had disappeared. Her little girl was turning out to be quite the charmer. She loved to clamber into her mother's lap and tell Catherine all about the antics of Buttons and the mischief of Scalawag, her small fingers curling a lock of hair on the back of her head. The talk on death did not appear to have had any impact on her.

Anthony, however, was a different matter. He turned away from her, as if she was already dead. Complaints began to issue from the preschool that he was hitting and spitting at the other children. He even reverted to wetting the bed.

"He refused his vegetables again last night," complained Miss Madison. "So I told him that he had to sit at the table until he had eaten at least half of them."

"How long did that last?" Catherine wondered at the willfulness of her young son.

"Until it was time to go to bed. I didn't let him have dessert."

"Good," said Catherine. "Tonight, we'll let them eat with us."

Catherine served asparagus and sliced it up for Charlotte. Anthony, however, said he could cut his own vegetables. Out of the corner of her eye, she saw him pick up an asparagus spear and slip it under the table. She heard Scalawag's dog tags tinkle in response to the offering.

"Get that damn dog out of the dining room." Catherine was furious.

"Catherine," scolded Paul. "Not in front of the children."

Catherine's foot kicked the dog. Scalawag yelped in pain and scurried out from under the table. Anthony began crying. Charlotte began to howl. Paul stood up and threw his napkin down on the table, glaring at her.

"I will not have dogs prowling under my table like sharks looking for food." She called for Agnes Madison to remove the children so that she could talk to Paul.

But he gave her a look of disgust and quit the table, his dinner half eaten.

"What's to become of us, Serena?" Catherine moaned. "A mother who is dying, a father who is drinking himself into a stupor every night, and children who are acting wild."

Only with Serena could Catherine let down her guard, confess her worries, and weep her sorrows. Every night, Serena would sit on the side of her bed and hold her beloved Catherine in her arms.

"Sweetpea," she said, stroking Catherine's hair, "there's a reason for everything that happens in this here world. We just got to figure it all out."

"Serena, all my life you've taken such good care of me. What am I going to do now? The children . . ."

Kate's eyes fluttered close. The book dropped to her lap.

Billy didn't notice. "Things jus' keep getting worser and worser in this story. It's a lot like my life."

"It's 'worse,' not 'worser and worser,'" Phoenix said.

"Yeah, it is,' said Billy. "My life is too getting worser. I got no money, no job, and no wife. Look at all the doo-doo I'm in. 'Scuse me," he said to Kate.

She pried open one eyelid and laughed. "The reporters asked Bess Truman if she could persuade her husband, the president, to stop saying horse manure. Mrs. Truman replied, 'If you only knew how long it has taken me to get him to say 'manure.'"

"Oh shit," said Billy. "There's a road block ahead."

Sure enough, all the cars were slowing to a stop. Police officers were leaning in the window, questioning the occupants.

Billy fished under the front seat for his gun.

"Put that away. You're going to get us all killed." Kate sat straight up.

"What am I going to do? What am I going to do?"

"Stay calm for one thing. Now put that gun back under the seat." Kate's voice was steady but in command.

Billy did as he was told, but he was sweating up a storm. Matilda crept closer to the roadblock.

"They're looking for me. I know it," he said.

"Maybe and maybe not," replied Kate, "but there will be no gunfire. Do I make myself clear?"

Billy nodded.

In the back seat, Phoenix bit her lip. It occurred to her if she opened the car door and dashed screaming to the police, she could end up on television. The courageous young victim of a hijacking, the savior of an elderly woman. Television announcers, newspaper reporters would be competing to get an interview with her. Maybe she could even write a book in which she elaborated on all the horrid details. Her fingers wrapped around the door handle.

"What should I do, Phoenix?" Billy whispered, as the car moved closer.

"Huh?"

"Should I jus' give up?"

All of a sudden, it became very clear to her that if she ran or he confessed, Seattle would be out of the question. The cops would simply return her to her mother. "Heck no," she answered. "We're a family, remember? You're my dad taking me to Seattle, to . . . a fancy boarding school."

Kate smiled. "And I had to come along, because this will be the first time you've left home."

"I don't know," moaned Billy, as he pulled the car up to the roadblock with its hefty policemen in tight-fitting pants and gun belts. The three of them unrolled the car windows.

Kate smiled benevolently at the officer. Phoenix tried to do the same. Billy just stared straight ahead.

"What's the matter, Officer?" asked Kate.

"A couple of convicts escaped from jail last night," he answered, peering into the car.

"Hi." Phoenix gave a little wave with her fingers.

The policeman smiled back. He tapped the car door and signaled for them to move on.

Billy just sat there.

Kate nudged him with her elbow, but he didn't move.

"Is there a problem, sir?" asked the police officer.

Kate quickly answered. "We're looking for the most scenic route to take north, and we don't quite know which way to go." She shuffled the atlas on her lap to indicate their confusion.

"That's easy." He pointed. "Just keep on this road and follow the Mississippi River. Great limestone cliffs."

"Thank you, Officer." Kate nudged Billy. "Time to go, son. We're holding up traffic."

Billy swallowed, nodded, and started the car forward.

"Oh, man. That was close," said Phoenix. "For a minute there, I thought you were going to lose it and turn yourself in." *For a minute there, I was going to turn you in.*

"There's the river on our left," said Kate.

"Why did you tell him we were heading north?" Phoenix asked.

"Because the officer might later recall our faces. I wanted to put him off track." Kate turned from Phoenix toward Billy, "Are you okay?"

White-faced, Billy shook his head. "My life's like that book. Things go okay, then whamo, you get the roadblocks. You can't go forward; you can't go backwards; and you know it's never going to work out. I don't know what to do." He pulled the car over into the breakdown lane.

"Do you want me to drive?" asked Kate.

He nodded. *Why drive anywhere when you don't know where to go?*

They switched seats. As she took the steering wheel, Kate's attention split into two: the rising cliffs were spectacular, but she worried about Billy, afraid he might be falling into another one of his black depressions. Time to try another tack.

"If the landscape were all flat, Billy, it would become boring, tiring to the eye. But look at all these green trees, the blue gray river, the valley carved by the water, the arboreal islands, the high bluffs that oversee the river. This is the high drama of Nature. It makes us want to see even more. Well, in the same way, a book has got to do the same thing. It has to keep the reader hooked and wanting more. That's the role of plot. If you look at most good novels, the progression is always from bad to worse. Conflict cascades through the canyons of all good stories."

While Billy listened, it was Phoenix who was taking in the lesson. "And we're not yet done with *Double Trouble*."

"Nor are we finished with this trip," Kate added. "You just have to have faith that things will get better."

"Happy ever after," echoed Phoenix.

"Sometimes yes, sometimes no. We don't always get what we want, Billy. You have to expect the unexpected. But everyday, each one of us is writing the story of his or her own life. How it progresses is up to you. It's the frame of reference that counts. You either learn from your mistakes or else you keep falling back into the same old story again and again."

"If my life is but a story," asked Phoenix, "can I change my past?"

"Nope," interjected Billy. "The past is fixed. Carmelita threw me out. Can't change that."

"Yes and no," said Kate. "It's a funny thing about memory. Your memory changes over time, depending on where you, the author, stand. If you're happy now, you'll remember more of the good times. If you're bitter, you'll summon up the darker images from your past. Conversely, as you inscribe the story of your life, the story will write you. It's something that modern medicine and psychiatry have forgotten."

"What?" asked Billy.

"The greatest energy for healing is the imagination."

Only now was Kate becoming aware of aches cropping up in ill-used muscles. Fatigue had settled deep into her bones. She needed to stop before too long.

Turning west, Matilda headed away from the Mississippi into rolling hill country and hardwood forests. It was getting late in the afternoon. They all sank into the silence of individual daydreams:

For Kate: *An hour-long massage, a warm bath filled to the brim, a red ball of scented oil, an old-fashioned novel of character, Gorecki's Third Symphony with its purring cellos. Sitting in a loose caftan, no restraining bra, sandals on my feet. A candle-lit dinner of light pasta and vegetables and someone educated with whom to converse. A companion my age. A gentleman.*

For Billy: *Opening the front door of a large, wealthy house, his mouth falling open with amazement, Phoenix's father grabs his daughter and welcomes her home. He hugs and hugs her, then notices me standing there in the background. He shakes my hand, asks my name. "You've brought my daughter back to me. How can I ever thank you? Do you need a job? Can you handle being the manager of my construction firm? Pays top dollar. Name your price. The job is yours, if you want it. Would you consider it? I'll pay for your move, help your wife get settled. She'll love it out here."*

For Phoenix: *Mom is crying. She's found my note by now. She calls my Dad. "Oh Jeff, how could I have been so mean to her? I didn't realize how lucky I was to have her as my daughter. Please, Jeff, send her home to me. I can't bear to live without her. I'll always be good to her, let her go to rap concerts with her friends, stay out as late as she wants. If she wants to go to Hollywood instead of college, well, that's her choice. She can visit you whenever she wants. Oh, Jeff, tell her how much I love her." Mom weeps into the receiver.*

A tear gathered itself in the corner of Phoenix's eye. She yawned it away, scrunching her fists into her eyeballs, and then broke the car's silence. "Every night when Mom tucks me into bed, we have this stupid ritual. Mom says that she loves me more than I could ever love her. And I always tell her that couldn't be, that I love her more than she could ever ever love me. We'd have this stupid argument. Well, not an argument really."

"Sounds like she's joshing you." Billy's mother always used to threaten to send him to a foster home if he didn't get his hiney into bed. He was so dumb then, he really believed her.

Indigestion rumbled out of the stomach area and hit Kate hard, like a balled-up fist in her chest, clutching tighter and tighter. All this traveling up and down the country was getting to her. Her head felt light. She thought for a moment she might even faint. "We have to stop. I'm too tired to go on." She pulled the car over.

Billy switched places with her. "You going to be okay?"

"I just need to stop for the night." Kate was determined not to burden them with psychosomatic complaints.

Billy began reading the signs on the road announcing the upcoming town of Northfield: "The Home of Colleges, Cows, and Contentment."

Phoenix groaned, "Oh God, another bovine metropolis." Ever since Kate had begun to lecture on stories, writing, grammar, and words, Phoenix had upped her vocabulary level to the max.

Signs to Carleton College and St. Olaf dotted the landscape. A small, bustling, river-college town, Northfield sheltered pizza parlors, banks, an antique hotel, stone churches, and college students.

"Hey." Billy grew excited, slowing down to read a historical plaque. "It says Jesse James was here in 1876 trying to rob a bank, but it didn't go as planned." He paused. "Kinda like what happened to me."

"Only Jesse James robbed the rich and gave a lot of the money to the poor," Phoenix said, "and you haven't given me a dime."

"I'm feeling poorly *right* now," added Kate, pointing out the College Inn where she had determined they were going to stay the night.

Billy pulled Matilda over to the curb. "I wonder if Jesse James ever got back home?" It was a rhetorical question which he didn't expect them to answer.

They ate a quick, indistinguishable supper of sandwiches. Kate ate lightly, her sole ambition to climb into bed. Billy wanted to walk along the Cannon River and contemplate Jesse James' forlorn end, while Phoenix headed in the opposite direction, up the hill toward Carleton College.

It wouldn't get really dark until later. The night was warm and touched by a lazy breeze, seductively cooling to the skin. As Phoenix ambled down a street bordered by middle class houses and scruffy lawns, she came upon a group of older girls sitting on the steps of a large house. She sauntered over in their direction. "Mind if I join you?"

They shrugged their shoulders and made room for her on the steps. "Where are you from?" asked a lanky blond.

"Washington, D.C."

"Here to look at colleges?"

Phoenix smiled. They obviously thought she was a good deal older. "Yes."

"This is a great school." The blond student flung her long, straight, gorgeous hair back from her face.

"But academically hard," said the short brunette.

"Come on, you've got to admit, this is a fun place," added the blond. They all laughed.

"So, your parents are driving you around looking at the schools?"

Phoenix thought fast. She didn't know whether there had been any publicity that she was missing. "My mother is dead, so my dad and grandmother are taking me on the grand tour."

"What other schools have you seen?"

"Carleton is the first one."

"Hey," said the brunette, "you don't need to see any others. This is the best."

A handsome young man walked up to the group. The blond made introductions. "This is Tom, And you are . . ."

"Daisy." Phoenix couldn't remember the character's surname. She punted, "Daisy DuMaurier." She waited with baited breath for them to scoff, but got no such reaction.

"Daisy here is looking at colleges, and Carleton is the first one," the blond said.

Tom squatted down next to Phoenix, beaming a perfect smile.

Oh, thought Phoenix, *I'm going to like this school a lot.* "Is it hard to get in?" she asked.

Tom smiled. "You need a high grade point average, but you probably already have one."

Phoenix melted inside. "Yes, I do," she lied. *And I will*, she vowed.

Down the hill, Billy stopped mid-way across a town bridge, spanning the Cannon river, and stared deep into the water's dark reflections. Despite his best intentions, he found himself unable to resist the pull of Carmelita. From the debris of leaf and paper, cloud and shadow rippling upon the river's surface, his mind conjured up her image. Driven by unknown currents, Billy trotted off the bridge in search of a public telephone.

Finding one, he nervously dialed the numbers, deposited the required change, and waited for her to pick up the phone. It rang and then clicked.

"Carmelita?"

"Beely, is that you? Where *are* you? Why aren't you here with me?" Her voice, like honey, flowed over him, lush and intoxicating.

"Did you get my card?" he asked.

"What card, Beely?"

"I, I sent you one." He forgot that he had only sent it the day before.

"Beely, where's my car? Where are my groceries?" The honey in her voice grew sticky, a taint of tartness. She didn't wait for him to answer. "Beely, you haven't gone and done something stupid, have you?"

"You really miss me?" He chose to ignore the impurities of anger creeping into her inflections.

"Beely, of course I do. Now when will you come home with the car and the groceries? I'm waiting, Beely. The fire inside me burns. You understand, Beely? I want you." She kissed slowly into the receiver.

It made him go all squishy on the inside and confused. He wanted her so badly, he could feel his toes curling.

"Bee-ly," she breathed into the phone.

"Please deposit one dollar and seventy-five cents," a mechanized female voice interjected. While Billy scrambled to find change, the dial tone resurrected itself.

"Gawd dammnit." He slammed down the telephone receiver. All he could find in his pocket were two damn quarters. The rest of his dwindling stash sat back at the motel.

Billy stormed toward the Inn, intent on reestablishing connection with his wife. But first he'd better check on Kate. He knocked on her door.

She was propped up in bed against three pillows, pale and looking ill.

"Do you need to go to the hospital?' She didn't look so good.

Kate shook her head. "A bad case of indigestion. It gets worse when I try to lie down. I've taken some anti-acids. That'll make me feel better in a moment. So what have you been up to?"

Billy looked at the floor. "I called her."

"Oh."

He told her about the brief conversation with Carmelita.

Before Kate could give any reaction, Phoenix sprung into the room, bounced onto her bed, rolled over on her back, hugged a pillow to her midriff, and gushed, "Someday I'm going to college here. But you have to study real hard, because they only take the top students. I mean, I may not have done so great in the past but that's going to change. Why study when you don't see any point to it?"

"And you have a reason now?" asked Kate.

"Yup," she answered. The image of Tom came to mind.

Billy started to leave the room. "Are you going to call her again?" Kate asked.

Billy shrugged his shoulders. On second thought, it was late, and Carmelita didn't like to be awakened.

NINE

SOUTH DAKOTA

The next morning, they awoke to a quilt of over-hanging gray clouds bunching in the west. Refreshed after a good night's sleep and a hearty breakfast, Kate was ready to renew the journey. Driving through the hilly countryside past Henderson, they watched the rolling Minnesota farmland progressively flatten. The road wandered past dairy farms into little towns sporting English names, such as Winthrop, Fairfax, and Franklin, until they came to the lonely outpost of The Lower Sioux Indian Reservation, a reminder of the country's earlier origins.

At mid-morning, the rain started to pelt the car in earnest as they pulled into Marshall with its generic shopping centers and fast food restaurants. Matilda turned south toward Pipestone.

"It's called Pipestone, because that's where the Sioux quarry the red, catlinite stone into which they carve their sacred pipes." Kate was an avid student of Native American lore.

"The peace pipe?" Billy's education came from watching Italians play Indians on television westerns.

"Only it didn't bring them much peace. It was upon these pipes the Sioux concluded several treaties with the army and the United States Government. Then the government system-ically broke every treaty."

"That don't seem right." Billy shook his head. "Every treaty?"

"Every treaty," said Kate.

"I'm hungry," interrupted Phoenix.

"Already?" Billy looked at her in the rearview mirror.

"I'm a growing girl."

"Yeah, and if I ate like you, I'd be growing too." Billy slapped his belly.

Phoenix could see that he didn't plan to stop teasing any-time soon. She picked up the book, frayed at the edges. "Okay, then I'm going to read."

"Aloud, please," said Kate.

Billy was curious. Was Catherine truly going to die or would her husband come to the rescue? That's what he hoped would happen.

Eleventh Month

From Catherine's early childhood, Serena had served as her self-appointed and under-appreciated guardian angel. This time was no different. Making sure that Agnes would double as a temporary nurse to Catherine, Serena unexpectedly announced that she was going to take a vacation. "I shall return soon."

"If you leave me with Miss Madison too long, I shall die a much quicker and more agonizing death," warned Catherine.

Serena did not inform Catherine, Paul, or the children where she was going or why. She bought a bus ticket and headed south, down through the lush middle-class countryside of Connecticut, past the overpopulated grime of New York City, the monotonous highway life of New Jersey, the industrial port of Baltimore, the Amish country-side of Southern Maryland, over the bridge into Virginia tobacco country. At Portsmith, she transferred to a local bus heading into North Carolina and the East Dismal Swamp. Bumping through the marshy country-side, the local bus finally deposited her at the coastal town of Belhaven.

Situated in the middle of town stood *Joe's Diner*, ready to serve those who had eschewed the grandeur of the Outer Banks for the more contained pleasures of the Albemarle Peninsula. A large piece of plasterboard, *Daily Luncheon Specials—$4.99*, tilted against the front window.

Serena breathed a sigh of relief. She had finally arrived at the right destination. Whether she would find what she was looking for was another matter. She picked up her small traveling bag and entered the diner. Might as well be now or never.

There, by the kitchen, stood Daisy precariously balancing three plates of luncheon specials on her arm, sole waitress, order-taker, and mopper-upper of the place. Joe roamed the back kitchen as the short-order cook. At first, Daisy didn't notice Serena, so occupied was she in delivering the food and taking an order from a couple at a rear table. Serena seated herself at a small window table. Studying the menu, she didn't realize that Daisy was headed in her direction until she heard Joe's voice.

"Hey, Daisy, there are other customers who need to be served first before that old woman."

But Daisy paid him no mind. She came over, order book in hand. When Serena turned to look at her, she squealed in delight and threw her arms around her.

"How did you find me? What brought you here? How did you get here? How are the kids, Anthony and Charlotte? Did Mrs. DuMaurier return? What's happened to Paul?" She plopped down on a chair opposite Serena. To hell with the customers and Joe.

"So many questions," Serena protested. "But he needs you. Even more, *she* needs you." Serena pretended for Joe's sake to be studying the menu. She didn't want to get Daisy into trouble.

"Who? Charlotte?"

"Catherine."

"Catherine?" Daisy didn't understand.

"There's something you need to know. Up to now I'm the only living person who knows it."

Joe stormed out of the kitchen and interrupted their conversation, "Daisy, what in the hell are you doing?"

"Jus' gimme a minute, Joe! An' if you don't, then I'm quitting right now."

"Okay, okay," he muttered. "Just calm down. I'll do the goddamn waiting and cooking myself, but don't take all day."

Daisy didn't give him a second look. "Go on."

Serena continued, "I was working for Catherine's parents before that child ever came into the world. What she doesn't know is that her parents couldn't make a baby. So they put the word out and found an adorable baby girl. The mother was poor, unmarried. You know how that happens."

"So?"

"Catherine was that adopted baby."

"You came all the way here to tell me that?" Big deal. Catherine could adjust.

Serena swallowed water from a glass. "That young unmarried gal had two children."

"Okay."

"Identical twin girls."

"Yeah? So?"

"Well, nobody knows what happened to that unmarried mother. Or to Catherine's twin sister."

"Yeah?" Daisy still didn't get it.

Serena wiped her brow. This was hard to do. She had promised Catherine's parents she'd never divulge the secret. She was breaking that promise now. Daisy had no idea what was coming next.

"The first time I met you, I knew, as sure as shooting, that you had to be that missing twin. Just look at you. You and Catherine be's the spitting image of each other. "

"You can't think that—"

"But I do."

Daisy sat back, stunned. "Mama never talked about me having a sister. She wouldn't have lied to me. No, you must be mistaken, Serena."

"Ask her."

"She's long dead."

"And the dead tell no tales." Serena leaned forward. "What about your daddy?"

"Never knew him. Mama said he was a lying, whoring, no-count devil. One night she jus' threw caution to the wind, and that wind took off the next morning, leaving her pregnant. Mama had to work two jobs to take care of me. So, you're wrong. She wouldn't have let go of her baby. She loved me like life itself."

"Enough to give up one to keep the other?"

"She'd have told me." Daisy played with the glass salt and pepper shakers, clacking them together, then pulling them apart.

"What about relatives? Aunts, uncles, grandparents?"

Again, Daisy shook her head. "Weren't easy being single with an infant. Family didn't want nothing to do with her or me. Said she had shamed them. She moved away. I don't know them, and I don't care to."

"So, there's no one to tell you the truth."

"I'm telling you. I don't have a sister. Never did." The thought of being in love with a married man was bad enough, but with her sister's husband? No way.

"If I'm right, and you're Catherine's identical sister, then you have the same rare blood type."

"So?"

"Catherine is dying."

"Dying? Of what?" Too much information was coming too fast. What was Serena saying? In her right hand she held the pepper shaker, in the left hand the salt. *One and one equals two. It's impossible. Improbable. One and one equals two. The bond of blood and bone. And brother-in-law.* Daisy put down the shakers and pushed them away.

Serena gently pushed the salt shaker back in Daisy's direction. "She needs a new kidney. She's going to die unless she can find a kidney like hers. An' if I'm right, then you can be that donor. You can save my Catherine's life."

It hit Daisy with a bittersweet irony. "Then Charlotte and Anthony can get their mother back and Paul can get his wife back, and nobody needs to be dying."

Serena nodded. She had said what she had come to say. Now the choice was up to Daisy.

Daisy shook her head. "It's too much. You really think that Catherine is my sister?"

"Yes."

"That Paul is my brother-in-law?"

Serena nodded.

"You know how I feel about him. So wouldn't it be better for everyone that I simply disappear?"

"Better for everyone but Catherine." Serena laid down the pepper shaker. "She'll die without the transplant."

"Why can't someone else do it? Surely, there must be others."

"By the time we find that person, Catherine will be dead."

"Daisy, hurry up!" yelled Joe from the kitchen. "Orders are backing up."

"I gotta go back to work." Daisy stood up. "What do you want me to do?"

"Take a blood test. Mamas can lie but blood always tells."

"All right, if that's what it takes to show you've been on a wild goose chase. Then you'll leave me alone?"

"Daisy." Joe's voice was insistent.

Serena resurrected the salt and pepper shakers. "Then you donate a kidney to your sister."

"She's not my sister, I'm telling you. Okay, I'll get the blood test. If she's my sister, I'll do it, but only on one condition."

Serena cocked her head.

"That none of them know who donated the kidney. Only you and me, Serena."

"Why?"

"'Cuz they'll want to thank me."

"I s'pose so. But that's not it, is it?"

"I can't stand to be around the children again, without them calling me 'Mama.' I can't bear to be around Paul, knowing he belongs to another woman. And if by some crazy fool of fate, she turns out to be my sister, it makes it only worse. So promise me that."

Serena had no choice. She had come south to unravel a secret. She'd head back north entangled in a new one.

"No way." Phoenix slammed shut the book. "I wouldn't do that for anybody. Let them pluck out a kidney? Gross. Nobody's going to touch my body."

"That's what all virgins say." Billy laughed.

"Are you insulting me?" Phoenix leaned over the front seat, trying to get into his face without hindering his driving.

"Oooh, touchy!" Billy pushed a little harder, convinced that this was the kind of teasing all females enjoyed.

"I asked you a question." Phoenix's lower lip thrust out. Her eyes narrowed into slits.

Kate could see that Billy was striding across a mine-laden field about to detonate. Phoenix was getting ready to clobber him. "Billy, you owe her an apology."

"Huh?" He glanced over at Kate, a stupid smile lingering on his face.

"Why do you keep goading her? Did you enjoy it when people teased you about your sexuality at that age?"

"Can't she take it? I'm just funning her. I don't mean nothing by it." The tenor of his voice was defensive, yet oddly challenging.

"Yeah, I can take it." Phoenix's mouth began to tighten again, a miserable compromise between what she felt and what she was trying not to feel.

Just as Phoenix was about to ask Billy what got shoved up his ass that morning, Kate interjected, "It's unhealthy. Far better to be straight-forward with others, say what you feel, rather than to insult them. If there's something that bothers you, then tell that person outright. Don't sit back like a coward, hiding behind sarcasm or teasing."

"Okay, okay. But truth is, I wish I'd never promised to take her all the way to the West Coast." Now it was out and in the open.

"Why?" Phoenix wanted to know.

"'Cuz," Billy answered.

Phoenix rolled her eyes, drew a deep breath, and tried again. "Because of what?"

He shrugged his shoulders.

"Perhaps there is something else you would rather do than transport a teenager and a very tired old woman cross-country?" Kate suggested.

Billy said nothing. A dark cloud outside opened up and started pelting the car. He stared at the road ahead.

"So?" Phoenix asked.

He pointed. A sign, *Welcome to South Dakota*, flashed by. "I'd rather be driving in the other direction. Carmelita needs me."

"How could you possibly think that?" Phoenix snorted.

"She said so. On the telephone last night. Or she would have, if we hadn't been cut off."

"Gimme a break." Phoenix grabbed her backpack and started gathering her things. "Carmelita wants a slave. I bet she wants her car back too. I can make it to Seattle on my own. I didn't ask you to kidnap me from that bank. And I'm not going to hold you to any stupid promise. Let me out right here, right now. I'll find a ride somehow." It hurt that he didn't want her around anymore.

"Can't. It's raining," he said.

"Hush up, both of you," Kate said. "Nobody is going anywhere out of this car. It's *my* car, remember."

Billy and Phoenix fell silent. The gloom of the gray outside insidiously seeped into Matilda.

With relief, they spotted a truck stop on the interstate. Billy maneuvered Matilda over into the parking area, opened the door and, without saying another word, headed to the bathroom. Kate eased herself slowly out of the car, her joints stiff, trying to find her balance. The rain spattered onto her face as she waddled toward the ladies room.

Phoenix didn't follow them. Lingering beside Matilda, she patted the right front bumper. "Goodby, girl. Thanks for the ride."

Once Billy and Kate had disappeared inside the rest area, Phoenix scooped up her knapsack and headed toward the big trucking rigs. Her plan was a simple one: she would find a driver who was heading west toward Seattle. That would solve her problem, and Billy could go back to Carmelita for all she cared.

The first trucker she encountered was a short, unshaven man with long, black hair, bulging biceps, a slick western shirt, dark glasses, and western boots, smoking an unfiltered cigarette and checking the lashings to the load on his truck. He took note of her knapsack.

"Where you headed?" he asked.

"Where you going?" she asked in return.

"South to Nebraska. Want a lift?"

She shook her head.

He looked her up and down. "But I'm sure I could make a special detour for you, darling."

"I'm going to Seattle."

"Well, that's a bit out of my way, but maybe I could find someone in Nebraska who's headed that way."

"You sure?"

"Anything's possible." He dropped his cigarette stub onto the pavement and ground it under his heel.

Phoenix looked back, checking whether Kate or Billy had emerged yet. There didn't seem to be any other trucks ready to roll.

His smile gave her the creeps, but what were her choices?

In the ladies room, Kate leaned against the wash basin, noting how pale she looked. It was lunch time. Maybe if she purchased a plain large pretzel at one of the food counters, she wouldn't feel so light-headed.

Billy had already carried out an order of hamburger, fries, and soft drink to the car. He drove Matilda over to the gas pump. Kate and Phoenix could catch up to him there. As he stood nozzle in hand, pumping low test gas into the old automobile, his gaze passed over the sixteen-wheeler trucks.

Knapsack in hand, Phoenix was hoisting herself up into a large truck cab. A man in the driver's seat was warming up the engine. As Phoenix closed the cab door, the truck began to roll out of the parking lot.

"Jesus Christ!" Billy threw a twenty at the gas attendant, jumped into Matilda, rammed in the key, and gunned her towards the exit, getting there before the truck. He slammed on his brakes, blocking the rig from leaving.

"Hey, whatcha doing?" the trucker yelled out of his window, gesturing at Billy. He wrenched open his door and jumped down onto the pavement.

Billy sprang out of the car, tense and ready.

"Get that old crate out of my way!" The trucker pointed at Matilda.

From inside the cab, Phoenix peered down at the commotion. When she saw it was Billy, she slumped down in the seat, as if to make herself invisible.

"You're not going anywhere with that girl," Billy said, keeping his voice calm and firm.

The trucker strode up to him. "You her Daddy?"

"No, but you can't have her."

The trucker slammed a fist into Billy's jaw and knocked him to the ground. "No little shit like you tells me what to do."

Rubbing a bloodied lip, Billy got back to his feet, hands up in a boxing stance. He danced around the man, looking for an opening. "I tell you that she's not leaving this parking lot." The metallic taste of blood trickled onto his tongue.

Like a miniature tank, the short guy moved in, landed a couple of blows, one to Billy's chest, one glancing off the left cheek. Billy staggered but kept to his feet. He tried to grab the guy, wrestle him down, but the trucker was a like a bantam rooster, small and slippery. He backed Billy up against the car.

"Come on, sucker. You want to fight?" the rooster crowed.

Billy drove his fist toward the guy's face, but it thudded into the shoulder instead, leaving his own face unguarded. The trucker's left knuckles zoomed out of nowhere, grazed Billy's right cheek, and burrowed into the bones around the right eye, followed by a series of body blows that doubled Billy over and had him gasping for breath. Billy reeled about, his arms flailing before dropping to his knees.

Suddenly a furious whirlwind hit the trucker from behind, pummeling him in the side.

"Hey, hey, hey," the trucker shouted, backing up. "Quit that." But the small fists and the raging female tornado, raining blows upon his ears and head, tripped him off balance. He elbowed Phoenix off his back.

"I don't need this shit." The trucker retreated back to his cab. Enough was enough. If that crazy girl didn't want a ride, why did she ask him in the first place? He floor-boarded his rig around the stalled car, the bent-over man, and the teenager standing her ground, glaring at him. She gave him the finger.

"Billy, are you all right?" In one minute, Phoenix had transformed from Madwoman to Madonna. She took his head into her hands. With her thumbs, she wiped away the blood.

"Oooh," he groaned. His right eye was swelling up. Two upper teeth wiggled in their sockets. Everywhere, he ached as he lurched to his feet. But, he had to admit, he was proud of himself. He had gotten the girl back.

Kate arrived, pretzel in hand. She studied Billy's face. "What happened to you? You've been in a fight. It doesn't look to me like you won. Why is Matilda parked out in the middle of the exit where she could get run over by a truck?"

Billy groaned and chuckled.

"It's all my fault. Billy was just trying to protect me." Phoenix's voice had that peculiar cloying sound, particular to females, a mixture of admiration and sympathy that makes a man's spine sprout a full inch taller.

Billy straightened up, surprised to find that he could take a deep breath. No bones broken. "It weren't nothing."

"Like hell it wasn't. You saved me. You're my hero." For a crazy instant, Phoenix wondered if she could fall in love with Billy. *Don't be absurd.* The voice of inner sanity snapped her back to her senses.

"But why would that trucker attack you over Phoenix?" Kate was clueless.

Phoenix shook her head. "The guy was just a real creep. Probably a pedophile or a pervert."

Somehow, Billy and Phoenix had come to a silent agreement not to worry Kate about Phoenix's decision to get inside the man's truck.

"He coulda hurt you, Phoenix." Billy said.

"I'll never do *that* again," Phoenix promised.

"That?" Kate knew she wasn't getting the full story.

"I'll hold you to it." Billy's voice assumed a more authoritative presence. "Okay, you two. Back to the car and to Seattle."

"But what about lunch?" asked Phoenix, scrambling into the back seat.

"Here, take my hamburger. Can't chew it. My jaw hurts. I'll suck on the fries."

"What I don't understand," said the mystified Kate, "was what the brawl was all about. It just seems to me these days that it takes so little for men to resort to violence as a way to solve problems."

"A man's got to defend his friends," said Billy, "and I count the two of you as my friends."

From the back seat, Phoenix touched Billy's shoulder in appreciation.

Kate smiled. For the moment, at least, there was peace in the car.

Nearing Sioux Falls, Kate insisted on finding the Public Radio station on the FM frequency. "It will take your mind off your bruises, Billy. Are you sure you don't want me to drive?"

Any other time, Billy would have easily given over to the ministrations of the two women, but he was riding high on his risen status. "No, I'll do the driving." His right eye stung like blazes. He blinked against the pain.

Kate took his soft drink cup and wrapped the remaining ice cubes in a handkerchief. "Here, press this against your eye."

One-eyed, one-handed, Billy drove. At least, the rain had stopped.

Kate turned the radio dial to a station crackling a spate of news. The announcer reported:

Now for the weird and curious stories. Last Tuesday, in our nation's capitol, an as-yet-unidentified Hispanic male from Miami robbed The National Trust Bank. Apparently suffering an unexpected bout of contrition, he chose to return the stolen money with an accompanying note of apology. The Bank has decided not to press charges. Charges from The District Attorney's Office, however, are still pending against the repentant thief.

"Hey, what about the hostages? What about us?" Phoenix couldn't believe that there was still no mention of the two of them.

"Why would the bank be willing to drop charges?" Sticky water from the ice cubes dripped onto Billy's cheek.

"Maybe the money I sent exceeded the amount stolen. I based it on their report. Perhaps the bank had exaggerated the amount for insurance purposes."

"But," Billy sputtered, "that would be highway robbery on their part."

"I'm sure they'll apply the excess amount to unexpected and hidden service charges. The interest rate on stolen money is probably pretty steep."

The radio announcer interrupted with the heralding of the next program *"Books In Review."*

Billy persisted, "But why do they keep thinking I'm Hispanic?"

Kate smiled. "The money was mailed from a post office drop in Miami. Don't forget, my friend translated the letter of profuse contrition into Spanish. If I don't mind saying so, it was a very literate letter."

In their own way, the teenager reasoned, both of them were true heroes. Kate had rescued Billy with her money, and Billy had saved Phoenix from the trucker.

"Listen." Kate turned up the radio volume.

Hello, this is Roger Eggler's "Books in Review" for South Dakota Public Radio. Today, we have decided to go, well, let's say a bit lower brow than is our typical fare. And let me introduce the panel of reviewers: Pamela Sharp from the Uni-

versity Extension Program, Tom Schocklethworp of the Dakota News, and Sydney Hassletwine from the Back Words Press. What's our first book on review, Pamela?

Why, hello, Roger. The first book emerges out of the romance genre. The book is "Double Trouble" by the ever popular Felicity Dare. The paperback is part of a series from Heartthrob Press and came out, with much fanfare, three weeks ago. As some of you know, Felicity Dare has quite a reputation—if not for her literary skills, for the fast-moving pace of her books. This book veers from her historical romance novels, as it takes place in more modern times.

"Hey, hey." Phoenix could barely express her excitement. "That's what we're reading."

"Shush." Kate waved her hand. "Let's listen to what they have to say."

Of course, many of our listeners have never read in the romance genre and have never heard of Felicity Dare.

But they should have. Felicity Dare is a hack writer par excellence.

Well, Sydney, I think that is a bit strongly worded. The book does verge on the mawkish from time to time, yet it is a story that keeps one's interest.

Yes, if you happen to be a hack reader.

Tom, what is your opinion of this book?

The theme of the double identity has, of course, been over-utilized in modern literature, but Dare is able to segue the story's identity problem into one of class distinction, elaborating it to more than simply a romance story. Of course,

Mark Twain did it a lot better in "The Prince and the Pauper."
Most of "Double Trouble" held my attention, but one irritat-
ing aspect kept pulling me away from the central plot.

What was that?

The characters were stereotypic to a fault. The poor south-
ern white trash girl, the rich socialite, and the southern
black mammy with a pseudo-black patois that can be traced
only to the cultural insensitivity of Miss Felicity Dare, who-
ever she might be. I would bet my money that Miss Dare is
white, blond, forty-five years of age, northern bred, filthy
rich, and racist to the bone, all the while publicly contribut-
ing to the NAACP.

Isn't that a bit strong, Tom?

Well, being a man, I don't know nothing about birthing
romance stories.

Well, there you have it, Roger. "Double Trouble" gets a
thumbs-up from me, a thumbs-down from Sydney, and a
so-so from Tom. Sales are showing that the book is making
money for Heartthrob Press, especially with the women
readers. And since the majority of fiction book-buyers are
women, I would say that the book is going to do well in the
romance market. Despite my colleagues' critical view, I think
Felicity Dare's prose shows potential for entering into main-
stream fiction. The problem, of course, with the romance
genre is that it is totally unrealistic. Life does not end up
'happily ever after' with all our problems solved by one true,
all-consuming passion.

Thank you, Pamela, Tom, and Sidney. The next book we will
review is "Stone Soup For the Chicken Soul."

Indignant, Kate switched off the radio. "Imagine, calling Felicity Dare a racist! She's my favorite author. I've read everything she has written. There's not a racist bone in her body."

"An' I like the book right good, although I'm not a woman." Billy said.

"That's right." Kate patted Billy's arm.

"What does 'segue' mean?" Phoenix leaned forward.

"Flows into, connects two disparate parts," Kate answered. "The reviewer is trying to show that Felicity Dare is using the conceit of a romance story to highlight the different values and habits of the wealthy from the poor."

"What is 'mawkish'?"

"Overly sentimental, insipidly sweet. I think the root word is 'maggot.'"

"What do bugs have to do with being sweet?" Phoenix was confused.

Red-faced with irritation, Kate muttered, "Racist, mawk-ish, hack writer. I don't think those men have any appreciation for the finer things of the heart."

Billy interjected, "An' it don't seem to me that the book is ending up so happy, you know, what with Catherine's kidney failure and all that."

"Well, the story isn't over yet." Kate's voice calmed down. "Pamela Sharp did have a point about romance stories always ending on an upbeat note. That's what the readers want and what the genre demands."

"But what if Daisy gave away a good kidney and then, later in life, got a kidney infection?" The idea of surrendering body parts made Phoenix queasy.

"She'd be up a stump creek," Billy said.

"I wouldn't do it. No way. Not on your life." Phoenix picked up *Double Trouble* and, as the car crossed the high, flat plains, resumed reading where they had left off.

Twelfth Month

Under the protection of anonymity, Daisy submitted to the blood and tissue-typing tests. The results were absolutely conclusive. A perfect match, identical DNA. There was no denying it now: Catherine and Daisy had emerged from the same divided egg.

"We found you a donor," announced the renal specialist to the DuMauriers.

"Who is she?"

"They don't give us a name, just an identifying number. The woman requested anonymity."

"But I'd like to get to know her," Catherine insisted.

"Be content, Catherine. Be grateful that they found you a good match." Even Paul did not know that it was a perfect match.

"But I want to thank her for this gift of life."

After two weeks of preparation, one kidney was, indeed, harvested from Daisy's body in a North Carolina hospital, quickly packed in ice, flown to Massachusetts General Hospital, and successfully transplanted into Catherine's body.

"Hell, this is gonna raise our insurance premiums, Daisy," Joe complained, having brought her a small basket of carnations. "What am I gonna do without you, while you recover?"

As she got stronger, her friends came to visit in her apartment, bringing her romance novels and Chinese take-out. "Why not try another fortune cookie?"

"No thanks," she answered. "One was enough to last a lifetime."

Over and over, she told them the story of her year up north, but not once did she mention that Catherine DuMaurier was her twin sister or that she had fallen in love with her brother-in-law. Some things were best kept in the closet.

Eventually, she felt well enough to return to her job at Joe's Diner.

The donated kidney worked beautifully. Catherine kept wondering about the anonymous donor who pulled her back from death's embrace. Life took on a new preciousness to her. Not a moment was to be squandered.

Her delicate beauty stunned Paul. Not only was she healthy again, but full of energy and purpose. A sense of personal power supplanted her prior discontent. Once again, he wanted to approach her, take her into his arms. and make love to her.

One night, he found her sitting in the living room, reviewing family photographs. He sat down next to her on the couch. "You amaze me. You're like a kaleidoscope of beautiful colors, constantly changing."

"Is that difficult for you?"

"Scary. I can't predict you anymore. It's as if you have multiple personality disorder."

She gave him an ironic smile. "Well, which personality do you like best?"

"I fell in love with a beautiful, mysterious woman. You were a goddess then, and I was your besotted human. That kind of crazy passion can't last, I know. But you're as stunning today as you were then." He touched her hand.

Catherine knew she was beautiful, but it no longer defined her as it did in the old days. "So tell me about these other personalities you have observed."

She wants the truth. I want to make love. He sighed and sat back. "After the children came, you retreated from me. Not cold, but distant, discontented, disconnected from me."

"From life," she added.

"Well, I didn't really enjoy that part of you. Then you changed again."

"How?"

"About a year and a half ago."

When I was in Africa. When Daisy was here. "Tell me more," she said.

"Well, you took more joy in the children. You were playful, down to earth. Even a bit flirtatious."

"A better lover then?" *How far did this infatuation go? No wonder the hussy didn't leave a forwarding address.*

"Catherine, that's a sore subject between us, isn't it? I don't want to spoil this moment with you."

"So which one did you prefer: the goddess or the earth mother?"

He sat back, thinking. This conversation wasn't going the way he had wished. "I worshiped the goddess, but I guess I fell in love with the more grounded part of you."

She stiffened and leaned away from him. "So that's the way it is. The goddess toppled off her pedestal."

"Into the poker games," he reminded her.

"Poker games?" *Just what kind of games did Daisy play with her husband? That little tart.* Catherine sighed. "Why should I care anymore?"

"What do you mean, Cat?"

"In the shadow of death, I've learned to fear nothing. I have no patience with pretense anymore, especially between us."

"We could keep trying. For the sake of the children."

"It's too late, Paul. Our marriage has lost that divine spark. It's a sham. You deserve better. So do I. Coming that close to death clarified things for me, forced me to see what is important. Being nice, polite, and doing the 'right thing' is wrong. I don't think I'm suited for marriage."

"But you can't mean that, Catherine."

"Oh, yes I do. I have a God-given talent for photography, for making the public see what they don't want to see. In my own personal life, I've been a hypocrite."

"But the children need us."

"I love my babies, but they're better off with you. You're the one who knows how to have fun with them. You're the one who most easily expresses affection."

"They need a mother."

"I will always be their mother. I will always love them. But the truth is that I resent them when they interfere with my work. It's better that when I'm with them, they have my undivided attention, not my annoyance." Catherine stood up from the couch. "Truth can be painful. But it's better in the end."

He bent over, his hands on the side of his head. The truth was too great a burden for his mind to bear. He wasn't yet ready for her newly discovered bluntness, smashing his dreams of renewal, filling him with sadness and anger. "But won't a divorce hurt them? They'll feel guilty that they did something wrong, that you don't love them anymore."

"No, it's you that I don't love anymore."

Inside, Paul shrank into an aloneness he could no longer afford to let her see. He looked up. "What happens next?"

"I'll give you full custody," she continued. "I don't need alimony. My inheritance and the commissions on my photographs will amply cover my needs."

Her sentences, so sensible, graveled ridges in his heart.

"I plan to take back my maiden name, Catherine Bristol. As soon as I can find an apartment in New York City, I'll move out of the house, but with one inviolate condition."

"What?" he asked, trying to keep the misery out of his voice.

"That you let the children visit me every time I return to the States."

They need their mommy, not a visitor. "Of course."

"I knew you'd be fair," she said.

"What kind of monster do you think I am, Catherine, to deny them their mother? Even if you choose to flit in and out of their lives, fitting them around your work schedule."

"I'm simply trying to be civilized here, pragmatic."

"Are you out of your mind? We're talking about your flesh and blood here. Don't do this to us."

But Catherine kept her word and left to find a New York City apartment. When she returned, they sat the children down and explained divorce in the most benevolent terms possible.

The children saw right through them.

"Mommy, don't you love me?" Anthony asked.

"More than life itself," she answered.

"Then don't leave me," he said.

Upon studying her father's grim and stricken face, Charlotte burst into tears.

Catherine left the next morning.

Phoenix slammed the book shut. "What a creep to take off that way. The kids are better off without her."

"To leave like that makes a person feel unloved, abandoned. So when do you plan to call your mother?" asked Kate.

Phoenix turned away and stared out the car window.

They drove into Mitchell, home of "The Corn Palace," a block-long building decorated with dyed corn and corn husks and murals of Native Americans chasing buffalo.

"Please, pretty please. They've got a museum and gift shop. I could pick something up for my mother."

"Nope," said Billy. "I want to get as far as we can today." The sooner he could drop Phoenix off in Seattle, the faster he could return to Carmelita.

Right before the Missouri River, the flatness gave way to small, curving hills and long fields of corn. High rolling bluffs emerged from a mist curling up from the Missouri River. "The Native Americans still swear that they can see the spirit of the buffalo running on these bluffs," said Kate.

Phoenix peered out. "I can see them. Really!"

Billy eyeballed the dramatic landscape with his one good eye and grumbled. "I can't see nuthin'. I think you're jus' making it all up."

Kate wiped away the damp streaks on her window. "Look at the tendrils of fog. You have to learn, Billy, to look with that third eye. Use your imagination."

Phoenix vigorously nodded.

Billy tried again, this time squinting with his swollen right eye.

Over the next twenty minutes the road rose gently to higher, flatter ground. In stark contrast to the verdant Missouri River valley, this land shriveled to a dry, corn stalk color.

Kate, too, grew paler and dropped into a highway sleep, the rhythm of Matilda's tires mimicking the lull of a lullaby.

Billy studied Kate's face in detail. Her mouth had dropped open, and delicate little snores issued forth. She seemed older, more fragile. When they arrived at Wall, the shadowy Black Hills rose on the horizon. Billy tapped Kate gently on the shoulder. "We can stop here at Wall Drugs, if you'd like." Had to be the biggest drug-store Billy had ever seen, a whole block long.

Stiffly, they got out of the car. As Phoenix cruised the tourist section of the store and Kate searched for indigestion pills, Billy hiked over to the prescription section. To a female pharmacist, he described the stomach pains and light-headedness of his eighty-two-year-old passenger.

"Given her age, I think I would take her to a medical clinic. You can never be too careful," she advised.

Billy shrugged his shoulders. Kate would pooh-pooh any suggestion about seeing a doctor. When had she become so important to him?

"It wouldn't hurt if you saw someone for that black eye of yours as well," the woman added.

Billy grew red with embarrassment. He looked around for his companions.

Kate had managed to arrive at the cashier's counter, arms full of bottles of Tums, Zantac, Mylanta, and Fig Newtons. Right behind her trotted Phoenix grinning and clutching a charger for her iPod, three cans of potato chips, two candy bars, and a bag of white cheddar popcorn.

Billy picked up two Ding Dongs, a hot dog, and some hot coffee before they climbed back into the sturdy Matilda. He gassed her up, and they took off toward the Black Hills and Rapid City. Soon, they came upon the dense pine forest, dark where the long limbs of the fir trees knitted together at the top. The landscape was fairly dry until they reached the city limits, where brooks, streams, and a man-made lake miraculously appeared to refresh their eyes.

Phoenix fumbled with her car charger, inserting it into an outlet and hooking up the iPod. For awhile, she blissed out on her rap music, bobbing her head and tapping her feet to the driving rhythms. But much to her surprise, she eventually found herself getting bored.

She picked up the dog-eared copy of *Double Trouble* and flicked past the remaining pages. "We're going to finish this book soon."

Kate looked at her. "Would you like me to read?"

Phoenix shook her head. "I'm not ready for the story to end yet."

"Well, I'm ready to quit driving. It's been a long day, and I've driven over five hundred miles." Billy veered off the interstate at Spearfish and headed north, looking for the cheapest motel he could find.

His stolen money had just about run out.

TEN

WYOMING

Next morning, following the peaceful Belle Forche river, Matilda crossed over into Wyoming. Phoenix picked up the atlas guide and begged Kate and Billy to take her south to the Devil's Tower. "Oh pretty, pretty, pretty please," she agonized. "It's where the aliens arrived on earth in *Close Encounters of the Third Kind*."

Billy shook his head. He didn't want to lose any more time.

When they stopped and ate a hearty breakfast at a truck stop, he simply drank coffee. He bought the cheapest loaf of bread and peanut butter jar he could find in the attached store. A person could go a long way on peanut butter sandwiches.

"But I may never ever get another chance in my whole life to see it." The pitifulness in Phoenix's voice spiraled like a cat mewling in the dark.

Matilda kept to her northern course.

Phoenix didn't give up. "We can listen to country music."

Now Kate was the one to shake her head.

"I won't ever swear again, I promise."

But nothing worked. *Sometimes grown-ups can be reasonable, but sometimes they're simply a real pain in the ass.* "Oh, read the gosh darned book then." Phoenix thrust it over the seat to Kate.

Two Years

Daisy returned to work, Joe's unwanted attentions, and occasional Chinese meals out with the other waitresses. She passed all her fortune cookies to the other women. "They jus' get me in trouble."

At night, her dreams conjured up Paul. She'd wake crying in her pillow. In her imagination, she'd work and rework their poker games, their lively discussions in the DuMaurier library. No one else had ever been interested in what she really thought. It was the greatest aphrodisiac she had ever experienced.

Joe just wanted to get her into bed.

Paul had wanted to get into her mind.

Then she'd remind herself: *Paul is Catherine's husband. Paul is my brother-in-law.*

Paul had given her books to read.

Joe gave her weekday mornings off.

"Be here Saturdays and half day Sunday. It's when I really need you, babe." Then he'd laugh at her embarrassment and give her a wink or snap of the towel. He knew better than to try anything more. "Sooner or later, you're going to fall in love with me. Sooner or later, you're going to wake up and feel lonely. Then you'll know what you're missing. Mark my words."

But she knew whom and what she was missing, and there wasn't a darn thing she could do about that. There was still her mind and it, too, was hungry. Every other morning, she'd bus over to Eastern North Carolina University to continue taking English courses. In Boston, she had discovered the pleasure of books, the joy of creating parallel universes with words and imagination, a gift she now recognized that was far more valuable to her than money. There was more to life than waiting tables in Belhaven.

Unbeknownst to Daisy, Catherine and Paul DuMaurier divorced. He assumed full custody of the children, while she received liberal visitations. Her career blossomed with a New York exhibition of her war photographs, fear and despair mirrored in the faces of frightened children. "No one can document human suffering as accurately as Catherine Bristol's camera. Welcome back to the world stage," wrote one reviewer.

Although well-fed and freed of parental battles, Anthony and Charlotte were miserable.

Assuming full custody of the children did not change Paul's work habits, so it fell upon both Serena and Miss Madison to take care of them. Miss Madison grew stricter by the month with no one to closely supervise her.

"Anthony, look at the dirt on your clothes. You look like a filthy pig. Take them off immediately. No, you can't go outside right now. Stop sucking your thumb. No afternoon snack for you."

"Charlotte, next time you wet your bed, you're going to have to sleep in it. I'm going to keep your baby doll until you start to behave. Now stop that crying. Only babies do that. Sit down and be still for once."

It wasn't so much what she said but the grating harshness in her voice that offered no love, no comfort, no reassurance to the children.

"I think you tear your pants on purpose," she accused Anthony.

The more she scolded, the stricter her commands, the more frequent became the bed wetting and thumb sucking.

Whenever Serena could get away from household duties, she pampered the children, although she had arrived at an age when taking care of them pushed her beyond what her old bones could tolerate.

Paul appeared oblivious to Serena's fatigue, the children's complaints, Miss Madison's short-comings. The divorce had seemed inevitable. So why did it hurt so much? For several years, he had fantasized about leaving Catherine, but now, stopping by the children's rooms at night, he found himself obsessed with memories and thoughts of her: playing poker, taking trips to the beach, kissing, eating lobster, singing silly songs with the children.

The women in his office invited him out to parties, to bars, and to their beds, but Paul turned them down. "I'm not yet ready to date." He knew whom he wanted: Catherine. And he couldn't have her.

Work became his solace and salvation.

It seemed to him that the household could run itself, until Serena announced that she was going to retire.

Billy glanced over at Kate whose voice was growing scratchy and tired. After he delivered Phoenix to her Dad, what would happen to Kate? Maybe this cross-country trip had been too much for her? It's not like she had planned to take the journey in the first place.

Kate's eyes momentarily closed.

An indignant voice rose up from the back seat. "Well who in the hell is going to take care of the kids?"

"The mean one. Agnes," said Billy.

"Serena can't leave," Phoenix protested. "Like this DuMaurier guy isn't paying any real attention to his kids."

Kate's eyes opened. Something in the tone of the teenager's voice alerted her that there was more to this than simple concern for Anthony and Charlotte.

"Phoenix, do you have your father's address?"

"Yeah."

"Current address?"

"Well, it's two years old. I think he's probably still there."

"You mean I'm driving you all the way out to Seattle, and you don't have a real address?" Billy shook his head.

"I'll call my Mom if he's not still there." Why were they all getting upset?

Billy looked at Kate. "Whaddya think?"

Kate shrugged her shoulders. "I'm not sure that any one of us in this car truly knows where we're going."

"Huh?" He knew where he was going, first to Seattle and then to Carmelita without reflecting that the two goals were in diametrically opposite directions.

Kate reached over and patted his arm. "I do believe that at the end of our brief lives, St. Peter will meet us at the Pearly Gates and ask us each a single question."

"What?"

"He'll look you straight in the eye, he'll look me straight in the eye, and he'll inquire, 'Was it a satisfying journey?'"

ELEVEN

MONTANA

"Why are we taking this road?" Phoenix asked.

"To catch Interstate 90," Billy answered.

"But we could have taken 90 most of the way." She jabbed her finger on the atlas. "It would have been a lot faster."

"Think how much you would have missed if we had taken the straight and true path," pointed out Kate. "Now we're in Big Sky country. Aptly named, don't you think?"

High prairie and sun-parched vistas greeted them. For awhile, all was quiet except for the steady thrum of Matilda's motor. Phoenix fiddled with her iPod, tapped her foot, and hummed softly. Kate's eyes fluttered and finally shut. Billy alternated closing one eye and looking out the other, trying to see where the buffalo roam. By letting his eyes rapidly sweep the grassy plains, he could briefly glimpse a herd of buffalo, a thousand-strong, grazing in his peripheral vision. But when he looked straight on, they vanished. *I could have made one helluva cowboy.*

Past Epsie, Ashland, Lame Deer, Matilda rolled westward like the covered wagons of another age, hauling her passengers to their unspoken dreams, unknown destinies.

Kate awoke to highway signs pointing to the Little Bighorn Battlefield National Monument. "Oh please, pretty please," she squeaked.

"I don't sound like that," the girl protested.

"Yes, you do," said Billy. "Okay, we'll take the self-guided car tour. I don't want to make any last stands here with park rangers."

Phoenix squinted at an historical plaque. "So who was this Lieutenant Colonel George Armstrong Custer?"

"A genuine American hero," Billy answered.

"Only in the movies and only in the Civil War." Scorn laced Kate's voice.

Billy shook his head. "Custer was the greatest of all Indian hunters."

"I think if you had studied history instead of watched television, Billy, you would have discovered that the man was simply out for glory. He graduated at the bottom of his class in West Point. In 1868, he murdered a large number of Cheyenne women and children, hardly qualifying for hero status."

Passing by location markers denoting where individual calvary soldiers fell, Kate added, "Here is where Custer's enormous ego sacrificed his own men. Right before he commanded his troops to attack Sitting Bull's people,

Custer's own Crow guides began chanting death songs. It took less than an hour for the Sioux to wipe them all out."

Phoenix grew pensive. "I'm glad I didn't live during those times. Think how long it must have taken to cross this country in a wagon."

"Shucks, you'd been easy pickings for the Injuns."

Phoenix glared at him.

Billy hushed up. Something told him that he might set off both females, and no man in his right mind would welcome two women on the warpath. No sirree. That was something this trip had taught him right well.

They stopped for a late lunch. Kate was relieved. She had found herself sweating more than normal during their stop at Bighorn. The next time she planned to go cross-country, she would either take the train or fly. It had to be easier.

After lunch and back on the road, Kate picked up *Double Trouble*. "Would you like to hear some more?"

"Whatever." Phoenix pulled out a fresh stick of gum, rolled it between her fingers, and popped it into her mouth.

"Shoot, yes," Billy answered. The experience of having a book read to him was a new pleasure. He'd miss it when the book came to its end.

Paul DuMaurier was dismayed by Serena's retirement plans. What was he going to do without her? "It will devastate the children. I'll lessen your hours, pay you double, give you more vacation time."

"No sir. I know my limits. I'm plain tuckered out. Time for me to go back home to Georgia, before I gets too old to enjoy it."

There was no changing her mind.

"How can we, I mean I, ever repay for all you've done? You're family to us."

"Take me home, Mr. Paul. I don't like to fly. I don't want to take the train. I'm too old for the bus. And I want Anthony and Charlotte to see where I come from, to meet my people. Family to family."

"Okay." Paul started doing the calculations of taking time off from work.

"But first, I want to travel some, see the country as we go south."

"A trip?" This was going to be more than a four-day, round-trip drive.

"For all of us."

"All of us," he repeated.

"Excepting Miss Catherine," Serena added, a sad note in her voice.

"Yes," he said. "To Georgia then." It was the least he could do.

Paul reluctantly arranged to take off the time. "I'll stay in touch," he told his office staff, "but I don't know how long I'll be gone." He granted Agnes Madison a much needed vacation, because Serena had made no mention of the nanny in her plans. Deep down, he nurtured a hope that during their trip south, he might persuade Serena that it would be better to live out the rest of her days with them.

"Perhaps things won't be as you remember," he cautioned.

"Perhaps," she answered, undisturbed by that notion. "On our way to Georgia, I want to see a Broadway show in New York City."

Paul made reservations at the Algonquin and bought four theater tickets, front orchestra. Nothing was too good for Serena, he reasoned.

For the show, Serena dressed in a bright red gown that highlighted her best features, her hips and bust, and camouflaged her butt. She insisted that the children wear their best outfits. "I don't want to be seen with any ragtag children."

The next destination on her list was Washington, D.C. The fatigue that had plagued her for months began to melt as they headed into more southern temperatures. The children found it hard to keep up with her. "Children, I want you to see President Abraham Lincoln because he was the one who set my people free."

After the Lincoln monument, she gave orders that they drive over to the National Cemetery to view the eternal flame above President John F. Kennedy's grave. "He talked of equal opportunity for all of America's people, not just those of pale skin and great riches."

"That's right," echoed Paul, momentarily reflecting, *What do I know about Serena, beyond all the years of service to Catherine and my family? A devoted servant, a wonderful person but not a friend. Who is she? Was it race or was it class that kept me from really knowing her?*

"Tonight, I want to hear the blues. I want the children to hear the blues. It's my kind of music," said Serena.

Paul took them to Georgetown's Blues Alley.

The children watched in amazement as Serena laughed and let loose. Paul had to admit that not only were the children having a good time, but so was he.

Next day, he drove them down into Virginia plantation country, stopping over at Civil War battlefields. Looking at the fields and woodlands, Serena told the children, "In the South, they'll tell you that it was 'the war between the States,' but my people know that the war was really about the evil of slavery. When one person thinks they owns another person, two things happen: one person may have lost the rights to his body, but the other has given up the rights to his soul."

Down into North Carolina, they drove under Serena's directions. The children complained of thirst. Serena consulted the map. "It says here that we're coming soon to a little town."

As Paul drove into the town, Serena pointed out a small lunch-eonette. "I sure would like a soda."

"Me too. Me too," the children cried.

"Okay," said Paul. He parked the car across from a shaded park. "I'll be back in a minute."

Serena took the children by the hands and crossed the road. It would be cooler under the tall trees in the park. Paul headed toward the dusty looking diner, a sign advertising cheap luncheon specials tilted against the front window.

"Here we are. Billings, Montana," Billy interrupted. A big city seated on the western bank of the Yellowstone River and edged by malls. They had no trouble locating a motel and an inexpensive restaurant.

"Not for me," said Kate. "All I want to do is to go to bed."

After a meal of pizza and salad, Phoenix and Billy brought back a melted cheese sandwich to the motel. They found her fast asleep. Phoenix whispered, "What are we going to do with the sandwich?"

"You eat it," said Billy.

Phoenix reached up and gave Billy a goodnight hug. "Thanks."

"For what?" he asked.

"For everything."

Billy grinned, although it hurt to do so. The edges of his mouth still smarted from the fight with the trucker.

Next morning, Kate treated them to breakfast. While she dabbed at her bran cereal and skim milk, Billy loaded up on flapjacks doused in a sea of syrup, and Phoenix inhaled three scrambled eggs, five pieces of bacon, three slices of buttered toast, and a large orange juice.

Barely two and a half hours later, as they headed into the lush valley scenery of Bozeman, Phoenix complained of hunger pains. They stopped for an early lunch. Kate drank tea, while Phoenix devoured a milkshake, two pieces of fried chicken, mashed potatoes and peas.

"You better quit eatin' so much or your daddy's gonna think you're pregnant," Billy warned Phoenix.

Her glance told him that he was treading thin ground.

"But, of course, you don't look really pregnant." He should have stopped right then and there, but something right evil kept egging him on: "Well, not much anyways."

Kate looked askance at him.

Phoenix didn't hit him. He was too bruised up for that. Instead, she bore her eyes into his and replied, "If my daddy thinks that I'm pregnant, then who will he suspect is the father?"

Billy swallowed hard, keeping his thoughts to himself for the next hour and a half to Butte.

"This place looks like the butt-hole of the nation," exclaimed Phoenix.

Indeed, Kate had to agree that the old mining town had little to offer: treeless hillsides, buildings that looked shaky to their timbers, and a couple of bars. Kate didn't know whether it was the heat or the depressing landscape, but her breathing came fast and shallow, as they continued to drive westward. Not wanting to panic, she turned toward Billy and, in a quiet, apologetic voice, announced, "I need to go to the hospital."

"You don't look too good, Kate." Billy stepped on the accelerator. At the outskirts of Missoula, they tore around corners, following the signs to the emergency room of St. Patrick's Hospital.

By the time they arrived, Kate was gasping for breath. Billy dashed into the emergency room, yelling for help. "I got an old woman in my car and she's bad sick with sumpin'. Says she can't breathe right. You gotta help her."

Phoenix tried to maneuver Kate out the car door, but Kate was having trouble with even that effort. An orderly rushed up with a wheelchair and picked Kate up by the armpits, shifted her into the chair, and wheeled her inside. Phoenix followed behind. A nurse intercepted her. "I need to ask some questions about the patient."

"Okay," she said, watching carefully where they were taking Kate.

"Name?"

"Kate Aregood." Phoenix peered down the hallway, frustrated that she couldn't be with Kate.

"Age?" The nurse was writing down answers on a clipboard.

"Real old."

"Are you a relation to her?"

"No. Well, yes. She's like my foster grandmother." The answer wasn't so far from the truth. "Is she going to be okay?"

"The doctors are examining her right now. Does she have any medical conditions that you know about? Does she takes any medications?"

"Um," Phoenix tried to remember what was the one pill that Kate took. "A pink one, small, oval every morning. And lately, she's been eating Tums and Zantac and that kinda stuff. I don't know about any medical conditions."

The nurse wrote: *Hormone pills? Anti-acids? Med hx unknown.*

"Can I go see her now?"

"Not yet," the nurse replied. "Tell me more about the symptoms and when they started."

But Phoenix couldn't really remember. Was Kate feeling sick and tired when Billy first kidnaped them? Or did that come later? She seemed okay at Niagara Falls but not so good in Northfield, Minnesota. "Um, about two days ago. She said she was light-headed, but today was the first time she really seemed to have trouble breathing. Maybe she's got asthma?" Phoenix knew several friends with asthma. She couldn't help blurting out, "Is she going to die?"

"You've come to an excellent hospital, and the physicians will do their very best. Now why don't you sit down in the waiting room over there? We'll let you know something soon."

After parking Matilda, Billy reentered the emergency room. "Where is she?" he asked at the desk. The receptionist pointed to an examining area, framed by curtains hanging from square metal rods.

"Can I?" Phoenix jumped up to follow him, but the receptionist shook her head.

The nurse returned with her clipboard. "Is that man her son?"

This woman and all her questions were really bugging Phoenix. She copped an attitude. "Yeah. Now can I go see her?"

The nurse looked up from her sheet. "Let me check with the physicians and see if that's okay with them. Agreed?"

Phoenix was mildly surprised that this adult, at least, was now paying attention. "Okay."

In two minutes, the nurse signaled her to come ahead. Kate was stretched out on a bed with a tube in her nose, the end of which was attached to an oxygen reservoir. Pale but at least awake and breathing normally.

Billy stood there holding Kate's hand. Noticing Phoenix, he said, "The docs gonna do an MRI on her brain and an ECG on her heart. They think she's having attacks of angina."

The nurse added, "We're concerned about your grand-mother's circulation, due to the swollen ankles, and we need to test her coronary arteries to make sure that they're clear and not blocked."

Phoenix checked out Kate's ankles. They didn't look any bigger than before. All old people have huge ankles, sort of like the baggy skin of basset hounds.

The nurse excused herself, leaving the three of them alone.

"I feel better now. I'm sorry about slowing down the trip," said Kate.

"Are you going to be okay?" Phoenix asked.

"Of course."

"What are we going to do now?" Phoenix asked.

"Let's see what the physicians decide. There's no good rea-son that the two of you should wait at the hospital. Billy, would you be so good as to retrieve my pocketbook? The hospital is most eager to see my Medicare card and supplemental insurance form. Then be off, the two of you. Find a motel for the night, then do a little exploring, come back in a couple of hours. It's too beautiful a day to waste by sitting in this hospital. I'll be all right." With a wave of her hand, Kate dismissed them.

Billy and Phoenix didn't have to wander far to find a motel, but they felt adrift without Kate. Their conversation was stilted, distracted as they were by their worry. Following Kate's instructions, Matilda cruised the Missoula streets, her occupants barely noting the big open lawns, the sporadic fences, the small mountains of the Bitterroot Range that framed the flat, valley city. Mount Sentinel hovered above the University of Montana campus, a big white-stoned *M* on its left flank, facing the city. North of it stood a large white *L* on Mount Jumbo. In the early afternoon breeze, Phoenix could make out hang gliders flying in the mountain updrafts.

Seeing signs for MacKenzie River Pizza, the two of them stopped off for a medium double cheese pizza with mushrooms, olives, and onions. But they both picked at the food and watched the clock and wondered if they had spent enough time away from Kate.

Finally Phoenix spoke up. "Think it's okay if we go back now?"

That was all that Billy needed. They left the half-eaten pizza with cash on the bill and headed out the door. When they arrived, they were told that Kate was still down in the MRI area, waiting for the examination. Three bitter cups of

coffee and two sodas later, they were finally directed to a hospital room where they found Kate resting, the tube still in her
nose. She looked annoyed.

"The cardiologists want to do an angioplasty which means
I'm stuck here for several days. I told them that I couldn't
remain, but they insisted."

"We'll stay too," Billy said. He couldn't imagine going on
without her.

Kate adamantly shook her head. "No, this is what I've
decided. You must take Phoenix on to Seattle to her father's
place. Otherwise, Billy, you're still at risk for a charge of kidnaping. I'll fly home when the physicians are finally finished
with me. You can drive Matilda back when you're ready. I
know she'll be in good hands with you."

"I'm not leaving until I know you're going to be okay."
Phoenix folded her arms in front of her chest and plunked herself down on a chair.

"Me neither," added Billy. "You're stuck with us."

Kate shook her head. "A compromise. I'm going to have a
telephone installed in this room. That way you can talk to me
AND make the journey west. Agreed?"

Billy wasn't happy with the plan but saw the wisdom in it,
nevertheless.

Kate turned toward Phoenix. "You can read *Double Trouble* to Billy and keep him awake during the driving."

Phoenix persisted, "But don't you want to know how
it ends?"

Kate laughed. "I already know the ending."

"You've already read the book?" Phoenix asked.

"I wrote it."

Phoenix and Billy exchanged puzzled glances.

"Yes, I'm *Felicity Dare*. And as you can see, I'm not blond, forty-five years old, or racist to the bone."

"Gawd almighty," was all Billy could utter.

Phoenix was totally speechless.

After breakfast the next morning, Billy and Phoenix headed to the hospital to say goodby. They carefully wrote down the telephone number in Kate's room.

"It will take you about nine hours to get to Seattle," Kate said, "and I want you to drive very carefully. Phoenix, you guide Billy with the map."

Billy interrupted. "I've been thinkin'. After I leave Phoenix in Seattle, I'm comin' back here for you. An' you can't persuade me different."

"And I'm going to call you every day," promised Phoenix.

"Come here," Kate commanded, beckoning the teenager with her finger.

Phoenix leaned over the bed to kiss Kate on the cheek, only to find Kate's arms wrapping around her.

Kate whispered, "Now remember, Billy still needs our help."

Phoenix nodded. It was a truth she had come to understand during the journey: sometimes adults were imperfect but that didn't necessarily mean they were inferior or bad or stupid.

Before they could make their exit, a white-haired man entered the room and introduced himself, "I'm Thomas Middleton, a volunteer here at the hospital."

"Your face is familiar," declared Kate. "You wouldn't happen to be the writer, Thomas Middleton? The one who used to pen adventure novels?"

He tipped his head. "One and the same. I didn't know that anybody would remember those stories. Or me."

"But they were wonderful!" Kate enthused. "Why did you stop writing?"

"My wife of fifty-five years served as my muse, and when she died of cancer last year, I couldn't write anymore. My daughter pushed me to join the senior volunteer group here. Said it would bring me out of isolation. So here I am."

"Well, we're jus' leavin'," Billy said, pushing Phoenix gently out the door and giving Kate a mischievous wink. "I'll be back with the car in a few days."

Kate called out to the departing girl, "Remember, be kind to your father."

But Phoenix didn't hear her. Already she was striding down the hall, heading toward Seattle.

TWELVE

IDAHO

Taking Route 90 out of Missoula, Matilda descended into an area where the hills flared open, grassy and green, then up the arduous road toward Lookout Pass, trees sprouting on both sides of the road. Up, up toward Idaho, the hills grew steeper and the views more constricted. Matilda responded confidently to Billy's steady foot. He didn't ask too much or move too quickly for her. He knew both her limits and her capabilities.

"What I can't understand," Phoenix ventured, "is why you plan to return to a woman who doesn't appreciate you."

Billy chewed on his lower lip.

"I'll admit," the teenager confessed, "that when we first started out, I was scared. Then I thought you were kind of dumb. But Kate helped me understand about learning problems, and the more I've gotten to know you, well, I just can't see you going back to somebody who treats you like shit. You deserve better." Saying all this, she knew, sounded sort of rehearsed, but somebody had to tell him the truth.

"Besides, you're my friend," she added.

Billy nodded. He'd been thinking the same thoughts. Yet maybe half of Carmelita was better than nobody at all.

"Kate thinks the world of you. She wouldn't trust Matilda to just anybody. She believes in you enough that she paid off your bank loan." *Well, it wasn't exactly a loan.*

"I'm gonna pay her back," he said.

"She knows that. She has faith in you."

Faith, what a wonderful word, he thought.

Phoenix continued, "A lot of respect, too."

Respect. A word that had been missing in Billy's world. He liked the sound, the texture, the meaning of that word.

Faith and Respect. He sat up straighter in the driver's seat, skillfully guiding Matilda over the high mountain pass, before descending into Idaho. If the truth were known, he and Matilda had a lot more *faith and respect* in each other than did he and Carmelita. He affectionately patted the wheel, holding the old girl steadily to the road's dropping curves.

"What are you going to do after Seattle?" Phoenix asked.

Before and below them spread a large valley, a view both dramatic and enchanting. "I dunno," he said, "maybe jus' follow the road."

Matilda sped down the freeway, over the old town of Wallace, past Silverton, Osburn, Kingston before climbing back up into the skies to The Fourth of July Pass.

Billy snorted. "This road is a lot like my life. Up and down, up and down, and a lotta downs."

"Kate says you have to have a dream, and that it doesn't matter if the dream comes true or not, only that it lead you somewhere," said Phoenix.

"Like a map, huh?"

"An inside map."

"Well," he said, stroking his chin while driving, "if I go back East, the F.B.I. may still come after me. And I don't know nobody on the west coast."

"You know me." Phoenix smiled.

"Carmelita doesn't really want me back. But where can I go? No place feels like home to me. Never has."

Phoenix understood that he wasn't asking for any pity. Billy was simply stating the truth as he had always known it. But his words made her regret the stupid, little note she had left her Mom. Despite all the strict rules, it was still home to her and always would be.

"You know what?" An insight struck her, something that might help him find his way.

"What?"

"The road goes up and down, but it also curves around, and we never know what we're going to see around the corner."

"Yeah?"

"So, you never can tell when, one of these days, you'll drive around that curve in the road, and you'll see it."

"What?" He didn't follow where she was taking him.

"Home," she replied, softly and with reverence.

Home. Yet another word to take in, savor, and add to his dreams.

THIRTEEN

WASHINGTON

Thirty minutes after having made the descent into the resort town of Coeur d'Alene, Matilda crossed the state line and cruised into Spokane. With Mount Spokane on the right, the city boasted several grassy hills, a profusion of pine trees, and a strip of stores. After filling up with gas, Matilda made another descent for about a half hour. The vista of trees began to disappear, replaced by a long, boring drive past big farms sparsely set off from the road, surrounded by fields of wheat, corn, and rye grass. A small line of poplars, used for windbreaks, occasionally dotted the otherwise, treeless landscape.

Bored, Phoenix picked up *Double Trouble*. "Can you imagine Kate writing this book?"

Billy chuckled, "Anything is possible with her, I've learnt."

"Learned," corrected Phoenix.

"Right. Learnt." Billy grinned.

Phoenix gave up. Billy was an original, and you simply had to accept him on his own terms.

"I wonder," she asked, "how Kate made it all come out in the end?"

"I got a guess. Remember she said that it has to end happy? An' I like happy endings." Despite Carmelita, Billy still believed in the promises and cures of love.

"Want me to read it?" Phoenix already knew Billy's answer. She opened the book.

Entering into the restaurant, Paul DuMaurier first spied a greasy-haired cook, stacking dishes in the back kitchen area. There weren't any customers. The waitress, seated in a booth and reading a book, had her back to him. He strolled up to the counter to order take-out drinks from the cook. He turned to look again at the waitress, even though he could only see the back of her head. There was something familiar about the set of her shoulders, the graceful neck. He caught his breath. If it weren't for the color of her hair, he could have sworn it was Catherine. Then she turned around in his direction. Oh my God, it *was* her. But what was she doing in this diner?

The hair style was different. The smile was different. But when she saw him, her eyes lit up. Not like Catherine. Like her and not like her. Like the way Catherine's eyes used to sparkle when she had stiffed him in a poker game. Like the smile which disappeared at the time of her illness.

She closed the book and pushed out of the booth, surprise written all over her face. "Paul?" she asked, not trusting her own eyes.

"Yes." He wanted to sweep her into his arms but held himself back. After all, they were no longer married.

"What are you doing . . ." they both asked each other in unison.

"Here?" Daisy finished the sentence.

"Looking for the one I love," he answered. It wasn't what he had meant to say at all, but it was the honest truth.

"But what are You doing here?" he asked. That was the true mystery.

"I work here," Daisy answered. "How is Catherine? Is she well?"

"What do you mean?" He sat down on a nearby chair.

"You don't know, do you?"

Confused, he shook his head. *I must be losing my mind.*

Daisy pulled up a chair close to him. "I'm not Catherine."

"Sure you are." He paused. "If you're not her, then who are you?"

"Daisy, Catherine's twin sister."

"She doesn't have a sister." This was a crazy-making conversation.

"It's a long story. You didn't really come here to see me, did you?"

He studied her face, not knowing what to say and totally confused.

"I'm the kidney donor. How is she doing?"

"Who?"

"Catherine. Is she okay?"

"Catherine is fine. She lives in New York. We're divorced. I have the children." It was all that Paul could manage. He recognized the eyes, the smile, but the mannerisms were not that of ex-wife.

"So you're the anonymous donor?" Paul was beginning to put it all together.

Daisy nodded.

"But I've met you before, haven't I?" He studied her face. "We've spent a lot of time together, haven't we?"

"Would you like me to rate those times on a scale from 1 to 10?"

Oh my gosh, he thought. "Playing poker?"

"It was a full house."

"Fishing?"

"Singing songs with the children," she answered.

Oh, my gosh. Oh, my gosh. "Making up stories for them at night?"

"And ones for you in the morning," she added. "Catherine hired me to replace her for a year."

"And I didn't catch on, did I? How stupid of me. I knew there was something different about you." He leaned toward her, his heart skipping a beat. "You rated marital satisfaction a zero, if I correctly remember."

She leaned toward him. "You were my sister's husband then."

"And you?" he asked. "Are you in love with anyone right now?" He knew it was impolite to ask, but her eyes pulled at him.

"Yes."

His heart sank. "Are you married?" There was no ring on her finger.

"I had stopped looking for the one I loved, because there was no way I could have him. There could be no substitutes for me."

She's free. Oh my God, she's free.

"Tell me about Anthony, Charlotte, and Serena. How I've missed them," she said.

"They're here."

"Where?" Her eyes wheeled around the room, searching.

"No, I mean, outside, waiting for me to bring them drinks," he stammered. "This was Serena's trip south. Ahh." Paul suddenly realized that it was not simply chance that had brought them together at Joe's Diner.

Daisy jumped to her feet. "I've got to see them."

"Wait." Paul grabbed her hands. "I have to ask you something first." He pulled her into his arms. "Am I the one you could not have?"

"I'm not Catherine, Paul." She stood her ground, not pushing away, not pulling him close. "I'm Daisy."

He wrapped her hands in back of her and drew her closer.

"You need any help there, Daisy?" Joe called out, concerned.

"It's okay, Joe."

"Do you remember the beach at night?" Paul whispered, mindful of Joe standing at the kitchen door, gape-jawed, staring at them.

"When you kissed me?"

"And you kissed me back." She wiggled a bit, as if to free her hands.

"I'm not going to let you go."

"You loved Catherine. You don't know me, Paul."

"Like hell I don't. I may not have known your name, but I know that I love you."

"I was trying to be like her. I can't do that anymore."

"I don't want someone like her. I need you, Daisy. Say yes to me."

"Well, that's putting the cart before the horse," she said, her eyes twinkling. "You gotta ask the question first."

He let go of her right hand and held on to the other. He dropped to his knees. "Marry me, Daisy. I promise you that by the end of the first year, you'll rate your marital satisfaction an absolute eleven."

"Daisy, you can't leave me," protested Joe.

"Yes," she answered.

Both men looked at her.

"Yes, I can."

Paul bent over and kissed her, the longest kiss that Joe had ever witnessed.

"Hey, Daisy," Joe shouted, "we treat our customers well, but that's taking it too far."

"I'm quitting, Joe. Right at this moment." Daisy yanked loose her apron and tossed it over the counter. Dragging Paul by the hand, she fled out the door, in search of the children and Serena.

"Oh, that's so neat," Phoenix said. "Daisy got her man."

Billy too was grinning from ear to ear. Paul had finally found the right woman to love.

For a while, neither one of them wanted to speak and destroy the magic of the book. Phoenix sighed, looked vacantly out the window while daydreaming of handsome movie stars declaring love to her. Billy tried to imagine what Daisy looked like. She sounded like his kind of woman.

Matilda flew by the Moses Lake area, a retirement mecca of tract homes and trees. The Cascade Mountains loomed in the distance. Finally, Route 90 snaked south along the Columbia Gorge, passing the Wild Horses Monument.

"Mustangs," Billy shouted, pointing toward them.

"They're not real," said Phoenix.

"Yeah, they are." Billy studied them. They weren't moving. "Damn! I wanted to see real horses."

"They're made of steel. Mom says art can teach us to appreciate what is beautiful in reality."

"I wanted the real thing," Billy said.

From the deep river valley, Matilda ascended into an open, treeless plateau.

"So, what do you think? Is *Double Trouble* real or is it art?" Phoenix asked.

"It felt real to me," Billy answered.

"That's what I tell my Mom about the few books I really love. Sometimes, I pretend that the characters are alive, you know, like family. And then, I get disappointed when the story ends, because it's kind of like a death, you know. Like they weren't real in the first place."

"I don't like endings."

"Mom's a social worker. She tells me that it's important to confront reality and not run from it, but you know what?" Phoenix had never confessed this to anybody. "Sometimes a good story is better."

"Better than what?"

"Better than what Mom calls 'reality.'"

Matilda climbed up to Snoqualamie Pass. Lush vegetation, ferns, cedars, hemlocks, shrubs, pine, and larch trees stood out in the misty atmosphere of mountain peaks and wispy clouds.

"Hey," shouted Phoenix, pointing toward rocky Mount Si, "Isn't that where the movie *Twin Peaks* was filmed?

"You think it's a real mountain?" Billy quipped.

As they descended down toward Seattle, a horde of cars flowed onto the road. City traffic.

"I hope you know where we're going," Billy said.

"I've got my dad's address, but . . ."

"But what?"

"I, I've never met him before," she confessed, darting her eyes away from Billy.

"What?"

"I've never actually met him."

"Now you tell me? Damn. Well, there's a first time for everything. Leastways, you've talked to him on the phone."

Silence.

"You've talked to him on the phone, haven't you? I mean, you told us how much he wanted you to come live with him."

Silence.

"Jesus Christ, Phoenix! You've never even said a word to him? He don't even know you're coming?"

The teenager bowed her head.

"Hell's bells. Now what am I suppose to do?" Billy was stumped. He wished Kate were there in the car. She'd know.

"Look, he's going to be real happy to see me, even if he doesn't know I'm coming. But would you stick around, just for a little while?"

They stopped off to get a coffee and a soda, gas up Matilda, and agree on some sort of plan.

"Are you really sure that you want to find your father?" Billy asked. "I mean, he may be right different from what you've been thinkin' all along."

"He's my Dad. How different can he be?"

"Okay," Billy said, "I'm gonna buy a newspaper and a city map, and you can direct us from here." As he entered into the gift shop section of the turnpike restaurant, a line of pretty, college-aged females chatted by the counter. There seemed to be a lot of good-looking women around this town.

As they climbed back into the car, the air was neither oppressively hot, like back East, nor chilly and damp as up in the mountain passes. What most struck him were the deep green lawns and parks.

"You see, it's got everything," Phoenix enthused. "Ocean, mountains, lakes, fresh vegetables."

"An' coffee places at every corner," Billy added. But he had to admit, there was something bracing, something festive about the city. Something welcoming. The city newspaper advertised several job openings for car mechanics.

Phoenix studied the city map. "Take a left here," she directed, "then another right at Ashton St. Go to the end. It curves around the lake."

"Whoa," Billy cautioned, "Jus' give it to me, one turn at a time."

Matilda wound around stately, tree-lined streets, where every house boasted a lush lawn and blooming flowers. Finally, Phoenix shouted, "That's it, number 432." Cement steps led the way up to a small, dark brown house.

Billy pulled the car up the hill, a couple of houses away from the one that belonged to Phoenix's father. "I'll wait here," he said.

"No, you're coming with me," Phoenix insisted, while performing some last minute touch-ups with her hair and face.

Reluctantly, he climbed out of Matilda, making sure that he had secured the emergency brake. He ran his hand through his hair, but he couldn't hide the black eye and bruised cheek.

Together, they slowly approached the house, climbing the cement steps. Phoenix politely knocked upon the door.

A teenage girl yanked it open and regarded them with indifference.

"Is this the home of Mr. Jeffrey Atherton?" Phoenix asked.

"Yeah," the girl answered, scanning Phoenix from head to toe. A couple of years older than Phoenix, she was also quite a bit taller. "What do you want with my Dad?"

Billy slowly turned his head toward Phoenix to see her reaction.

"Your dad's an old friend of my mother, and she told me to look him up," Phoenix replied.

"D-a-a-d," the older teenager yelled back into the dark interior of the house. "Somebody's here to see you." She left them at the door and vanished back into the house.

Phoenix swallowed hard, trying to assimilate the fact that her father had a whole other family.

"This is getting kinda thick," whispered Billy. "I'm gonna go and lean against Matilda. If you need me, call me." He didn't think it wise to be too close to Phoenix's father when she told him who she really was. The man might get to asking too many questions about how his daughter ended up on his doorstep.

Phoenix sat down on the top step and watched Billy's retreating back.

"Hello?" From behind her, a man's voice spoke.

Phoenix twisted her head and was about to stand up, when the man motioned for her to keep her seat. A nice-looking man of medium build and a shock of wavy brown hair. Phoenix couldn't immediately discern any real family resemblance.

"Judy tells me that I know your mother."

Phoenix nodded. "Shirley Knott."

He had to think a moment. "Long time ago. We were in graduate school together, planning to save the world as social workers." He laughed.

"She still is a social worker."

"Oh?"

"Washington, D.C. She works with the homeless."

"That sounds like Shirley. Those were wild days then. We never did save the world. I had a daughter at that time and burgeoning responsibilities. Life began to get increasingly serious."

"A daughter?" *Is he talking about me?*

"In fact, you just met her. Judy."

"Oh." Phoenix plastered a smile on her face. "Did you have any other children?"

"None that I know about. Why?"

Phoenix recovered. "Mom likes news of her old friends."

"Is that your boyfriend over there?" He nodded towards Billy leaning against the car door.

She was pretty sure that he was teasing her, but she didn't think it at all funny. "No, that's my father. Anyways, I better get going. I'll tell Mom I saw you." She stood up and shook his hand.

"Tell her I send my regards." He hooked his thumb in Billy's direction. "Shirley married that guy?"

"Oh, they've been divorced a long time. Ever since I can remember." Phoenix descended the stairs. She turned and waved goodby.

Jeffrey Atherton stood there, a puzzled look on his face as he watched the strange girl depart and the even stranger guy standing by the old car. "Tell Shirley to give me a call sometime," he yelled.

Billy was studying the Seattle map when Phoenix walked up to him. "How did it go?"

Phoenix shook her head. "I don't know who that guy was, but he wasn't my father, that's for sure."

"Right name and address."

"Look, believe me, Billy. That man was not my father. Now, come on, let's get out of here." She jumped into the front seat.

Despite his confusion, Billy knew that it was better to leave well enough alone. He climbed into the car and handed the map to Phoenix. "Where to?"

"Turn back out onto the main street. I need to find a telephone," she said.

A few blocks away, Matilda pulled alongside an outside pay telephone and stopped. Billy watched Phoenix head for the phone. A few minutes later, she returned, oddly content.

"I called my Mom collect," she explained, slamming shut the door. "You know what she said? She wasn't worried about me, knew I was safe on this trip all along."

"I'd thought she'd been hysterical, you being kidnaped and all that."

"She doesn't really know about that part. At Niagara Falls, Kate sent Mom a postcard saying she had met me in D.C. and thought it safer that I travel with her, that she'd look out after me and keep my mother informed of our progress. Kate promised she would deliver me safely to Seattle. That we were both on an adventure. Can you believe that?"

"An adventure?" Billy's mouth dropped open.

"All along the trip, she's been sending my mother postcards, saying what fun we were having. Niagara Falls, the ferry boat, Wisconsin Dells, you name it. She even sent Mom a postcard of Sitting Bull."

"Sounds like Kate's done saved you a lot of grief. "What did she say 'bout me in them postcards?"

"She didn't," Phoenix answered.

"Huh?"

"Kate didn't say anything about you or how she was so ancient."

Billy didn't know whether to be hurt or relieved.

"Mom thinks that Kate is in her late twenties, you know, single and able to take off on crazy cross-country trips. She said she'd send me an airplane ticket to fly home, but I told her that I couldn't leave yet, that I'd call her back later."

"Oh?"

"I want to go back to Missoula. I owe Kate that. I can fly out of there as easily as out of Seattle."

"But wasn't your mamma angry at you for running off?"

"Yes, but you know something? She told me she had done the same thing at my age. Snuck off to the beach for five days with a friend. Scared her parents shitless, but it was one of the best times she ever had. I promised her I wouldn't do it again."

"Sounds like a helluva good mom to me."

"I told her about meeting that man, Jeffrey Atherton."

"Yeah? What did she say to that?"

"She told me that we'd have to sit down when I get home and have a long talk."

"That's for sure."

"You know, Billy?" Phoenix turned toward him. "I've learned three things on this trip."

"Like what?"

"What love is, what's really important, and that things aren't always what they appear to be or what you want them to be."

Billy whistled. "I'd say you learnt a lot."

"That's exactly what Mom said."

"Nah, I betcha your Mom said 'learned.'" Billy nudged Phoenix on the arm, and they both laughed.

Phoenix agreed to study the map, while Billy took his turn at the telephone. He pulled Kate's scrawled telephone number out of his pocket. It rang a good long time before a male voice answered.

"Hello, is Kate okay?" Billy was worried.

"Who is this?"

"Family," Billy answered.

"Yes, I think we've already met. I'm the volunteer. Kate had the angioplasty this morning. She's still down in the recovery area but doing well. Perhaps you'd like to leave her a message?"

Billy paused. "Tell her that Phoenix met her dad and she says he isn't her dad and that she called her Mom and found out about the postcards."

"If you could talk a little slower, I could write this all down."

"Oh, forget all that. Jus' tell her that we haven't finished the story yet." Billy replaced the telephone receiver on the cradle and headed back to the car.

"Is she okay?" Phoenix asked, looking up from the map.

"I think so."

"One last thing, before we head back over to Montana," Phoenix said.

"What now?"

"You wanted to see the water, and I can direct us there. Okay?" She traced the route on the city map with her finger.

It sounded good to him. Off Matilda headed, toward the water's edge and a late afternoon view of the western sun.

"Oh, and one more thing," Phoenix added. "I need to buy my Mom a picture postcard of the Pacific Ocean."

F O U R T E E N

MISSOULA

"*Well, are you ready?*" asked Phoenix. As they retraced their steps east along route 90, the sky was growing darker. It would be night before long.

"Ready for what?"

"To hear the end of the story. We're running out of pages."

Phoenix picked up the battered copy of *Double Trouble*.

Billy settled back into his seat, keeping his eyes on the road. He didn't know whether he would drive all night or whether they would have to stop along the way. If he got sleepy, he'd suggest that they sleep in the car because his cache of money was about exhausted. He didn't have anything left with which to start a new life.

"No," he said. "I want Kate to read the ending."

"But she already knows it. It's her story."

"No, it's not," he said. "It's your story, and it's my story."

Billy felt oddly content. Serena was headed for Georgia and a peaceful retirement. Paul, Daisy and the children would return to Boston for a long and happy marriage. And he, William Tyler Pickle, would take his chances in Seattle. Lots of jobs for mechanics there. Lots of pretty girls. Paul got divorced and survived. So could he. After leaving Matilda with Kate, he'd take a bus back from Missoula. Find employment, buy a second-hand car and fix her up, drink a lot of Seattle coffee, and maybe get a girl.

Matilda sliced through the night, following the interstate up into the mountains and down into the valleys. Not once did they stop, except to go the bathroom and gas up the car. Phoenix leaned her head against the back of her seat, but when she had fallen deep into sleep, her head bobbled and rolled over onto Billy's right shoulder.

He smiled and lowered his shoulder, so that it would make for a more comfortable perch. He added being a daddy to his dream of the future.

Idaho gave way to Montana, and finally the lights of Missoula appeared ahead. Billy found their old motel and rented a room from a sleepy clerk. He half-carried, half-dragged the weary Phoenix into the room. She flopped down on the bed and promptly returned to sleep. He tucked her into the bed, smoothed the hair off her face, then took a long shower and put on a pair of clean underwear, before sinking into the other bed. When he awoke, Phoenix was gone.

"Ah Jeez," he swore. What a time for her to take off. He looked out the door, but there was no sign of the girl. What would he tell Kate?

Running his hands through his hair, Billy knew he looked grizzled and unkempt, standing partway out the door, his feet bare, in his jockey shorts, his beard with a good's day growth. He shaved his face, found a rumpled but clean shirt, socks, and pants. He dressed and sat down on the bed, trying to figure out what to do next.

The door handle twisted. In strolled Phoenix, carrying two enclosed Styrofoam plates of breakfast goodies. She grinned at him. "Guess what I got?" Opening up the white boxes, Phoenix revealed scrambled eggs, bacon, biscuits. "We can make coffee here in the motel," she said. She tossed him a cellophane-wrapped plastic fork and knife.

His eyes still wide with surprise, Billy didn't know what to say.

"Thank you? Hello? I appreciate you're getting my breakfast?" Phoenix was full of suggestions.

"I thought you'd run away again," he answered, embarrassed by his lack of faith in her.

"Now why would you think that? I'm not stupid, you know."

"Phoenix . . ." he began.

"Yes?"

"Thanks for the food."

"You're welcome."

By the time they reached the hospital, it was almost noon. They took the elevator up to Kate's floor. As they approached her room, they could hear the sound of laughter.

Kate was sitting up in the bed, glowing. In a chair, facing her, sat Thomas Middleton in the middle of a long, humorous story. "But you won't believe what happened next . . . ."

When Phoenix and Billy made their entrance, Thomas stood up. Phoenix planted a big kiss on Kate's right cheek, as did Billy on her left one. Kate took their hands. "Do tell me about your adventures in Seattle. I want to hear all about them."

Thomas offered to leave, but Kate ordered him to sit back down and stay. Phoenix perched on one side of the bed, while Billy stood by the other side. She told Kate everything: about the man with her father's name, the girl, the telephone call to her mother, the trip to Puget Sound, and her plan to fly home from Missoula.

Kate carefully listened. When Phoenix had finished, Kate turned toward Billy. "I'm proud of the way you watched over her."

Billy beamed.

"And what are your plans?" Kate asked. "Have you made a dream for yourself?"

Billy nodded. "I'm gonna take the bus back to Seattle, get a job as a mechanic." He hesitated a second, then added, "an' get a divorce from Carmelita."

Kate nodded in approval. "Seattle is a wonderful place to call home."

"But how are you gonna get Matilda back to the east coast?"

"I wanted to talk to you about that, Billy. Like you, I'd gotten into a rut with my life. *Double Trouble* was going to be my last romance novel. I wanted to write something different, more adventurous. That's why I accepted your invitation to travel across this great country."

Obviously, she had not divulged either the bank robbery or the hostage situation to Mr. Middleton.

"One adventure leads to another," Kate continued, "and Thomas here has suggested that we write a novel together. Of course, that would mean that I would move out here to Missoula and explore some of the wild west with him."

Phoenix's mouth dropped open. It didn't seem quite decent for someone of Kate's age to suddenly drop her old life for a new one with a complete stranger.

Kate squeezed her hand. "At my age, dear, one can't tarry too long in indecision. Life passes by much too quickly."

"But what about the cat?"

"Poofie?"

Phoenix nodded.

"I suspect that Poofie has been having a wonderful time roaming and terrorizing the neighborhood while I've been away. Thomas is allergic to cats, and frankly, I've not missed Poofie for a minute. Does that shock you?"

"But he'll be homeless," Phoenix protested.

"Not if you'll take care of him," Kate suggested. "That is, if we can find him. Thomas has agreed to fly back with me, when I'm fully recovered, to help pack up the townhouse and put it on the market."

"Okay. I'll take Poofie." It struck Phoenix that maybe she could open a shelter for homeless animals.

"As for you, Billy," Kate continued, "I want to sell Matilda to you for a dollar. I can't imagine that she could find anybody who could take better care of her."

"But I already owe you a lot of money."

"Don't worry. You'll pay me all that money back in time. I have no immediate need for it. I expect you to drive over the mountains to Missoula from time to time to let me see Matilda occasionally."

"I'll take real good care of her."

"Can I come too?" Phoenix asked. Maybe her mother would let her fly out to see Kate next summer.

"Absolutely." Kate shook her finger at each one of them. "I will be very disappointed if we don't have a least one annual reunion for the rest of our lives."

"If you two know what is good for you, you'll obey her wishes," Thomas Middleton observed.

Phoenix and Billy nodded. They knew only too well the strong will that lurked behind her gentle exterior.

"I can feel the muse already returning to my soul," Thomas added, "and if I swear to utter secrecy, Kate promises to tell me a story about the three of you that, she says, I'll never believe."

"One last thing," said Kate. "I want to know your reaction to *Double Trouble*?"

Phoenix pulled out the book and handed it to her. "We couldn't finish it without you."

Kate clapped her hands in delight. "Phoenix, why don't you read the last pages to us?"

Phoenix shook her head. "We want you to read it."

"Well, I must warn you then. Every ending is but a new beginning." Kate opened the book and cleared her throat.

Daisy spied the children before they saw her. She dropped Paul's hand and tore across the street, whooping and hollering with glee. "Anthony! Charlotte!"

The children scrambled off the park bench and bolted towards her, like two exuberant puppies let out of their cages. "Mom!" they cried, grabbing onto her skirt and hugging her from all sides. Serena followed closely behind. Daisy kissed the children, then flung her arms around Serena. "You devil, you."

"I was just doing what made sense, Daisy," Serena answered.

"Daisy?" Anthony looked up, puzzled.

"Aunt Daisy to you, little one." Paul tousled his hair. "The reason you thought she was your momma is because she's your momma's twin sister."

Charlotte backed away a moment to study Daisy. The hair was different, shorter and darker in color, but otherwise she looked just like her mother.

Daisy knelt down on the grass. "You're scaring the children, Paul." She put out her arms and gathered the two youngsters close to her. "I'm no stranger to you. Remember when we drove up to Maine?"

"And ate lobster?" Anthony interjected.

"And sang songs together," Daisy continued. She turned toward the newly bashful Charlotte. "At night I told you stories so you would go to sleep and not be scared of the dark."

Charlotte's body still held stiff, reserved.

"The first time I met you, Charlotte," Daisy recalled, "was in the garden. Your ball rolled into the pond."

"You got all wet," Charlotte shouted.

"Well, I came to stay with you at that time for many months, while your mother was away. Because she loved you so much, your mother asked me to pretend to be her, so that you wouldn't get upset and be lonely without her. Then she got sick, and that's when she came back home."

"And because she's your mother's twin sister," Paul reiterated, "she looks just like your mother, but she's really your aunt."

"Aunt Daisy?" Anthony rolled the strange words over his tongue.

Paul knew this was confusing. He sat down on the grass to talk to them on their level. "Darlings, Aunt Daisy came to help us when your Mom went away. Now Serena wants to go home, and we've got to let her go home." The children looked up at Serena, with worry more than sadness etched into their faces. But they paid close attention, because their father was using his I've-Got-Something-Very-Important-To-Tell-You voice. Without any notice, Charlotte slipped her hand into Daisy's hand.

Paul continued, "After your mother and I got divorced, I became terribly sad. All of us hurt inside. We've stumbled along, with the help of Serena and Miss Madison."

Anthony screwed up his face at the mention of Miss Madison.

"So I've made a big decision." Paul looked at his children. "I've asked Daisy, your aunt, to marry me, and she has said yes."

"Hallelujah! Hallelujah! Thank you, Jesus!" shouted Serena, throwing up her arms.

Charlotte's eyes grew wide and happy.

Anthony studied his father's face for reaction.

Paul took Daisy's one free hand. Again, he spoke to the children, "Daisy will now become your stepmother."

"Can I call her Momma?" Charlotte asked.

Paul deferred to Daisy.

Daisy answered, "You can call me whatever you wish. What do you call your mother?"

"Mom," said Anthony.

"Then 'Momma' will be perfectly fine with me. When I met you, I fell in love with the two of you, as if you had been my own children. I will always love you, play with you, tell you stories, and sing you songs. We won't forget to give thanks to your mother, my sister, for letting me become part of your family. Is that understood?" Somehow Daisy sensed it was important for the children to know that she would never try to usurp their mother's position.

The children solemnly nodded.

"And one more thing," Daisy added, looking straight into the children's eyes. "There will be no more divorces in this family."

Paul reached over and kissed her.

Ten minutes later, they arrived at Daisy's small apartment in Belhaven. She quickly packed her bags, gathered up her books and notebooks, and took one last look at her old life before shutting the door. They stopped off at the post office to leave a forwarding address.

"Then it's off we go to Georgia and Serena's home," announced Paul.

Frowning, Daisy emerged from the post office, an envelope in her hand. She climbed into the front seat of the car.

"What's that?" teased Paul, "A letter from an old boyfriend?"

Daisy shook her head. The postmark read *New York City*. "It's from a publishing house. I don't know if I dare open it."

"Why's that?" Serena leaned forward from her position in the back seat, between the children.

"You're going to think this silly, but I was so lonely for you guys, I took a writing class and . . ."

"And what?" Paul noticed her hands worrying the envelope.

Daisy blurted out, "I wrote a novel and sent it out to publishers. This is my first letter back."

"Go ahead and open it," urged Paul.

"But it might be a rejection letter." She wavered.

"Go ahead. Today is our lucky day," he said.

Daisy ripped open the letter and started whooping in glee. "I can't believe it. They said yes."

They made her read the letter three times in succession.

"Am I in the novel?" Anthony wanted to know.

Daisy shook her head. "It's not that kind of story."

"Well, what kind of story is it?" Paul asked. "Why don't you read us a little bit of it?"

"I don't know," Daisy hesitated. "You really want to hear the beginning of it?"

They all nodded.

Daisy dug into her papers and found the manuscript. "Well, here goes," she began:

It was one of those days when nothing goes right. One of those days when the wind throws grit into the human eye, and in a blink, the world shifts and shivers, and nothing is the same as it was. When life itself blurs out of focus, and in the void, echoes the great belly laugh of the universe.

THE END